D0366474

torn to pieces

margot mcdonnell

torn

to pieces

DELACORTE PRESS

Copyright © 2008 by Margot McDonnell

All rights reserved. Published in the United States by Delacorte Press, an imprint of Random House Children's Books, a division of Random House, Inc., New York. Originally published in hardcover in the United States by Delacorte Press in 2008.

Delacorte Press is a registered trademark and the colophon is a trademark of Random House, Inc.

Visit us on the Web! www.randomhouse.com/teens

Educators and librarians, for a variety of teaching tools, visit us at www.randomhouse.com/teachers

The Library of Congress has cataloged the hardcover edition of this work as follows:
McDonnell, Margot.
Torn to pieces / Margot McDonnell.
p. cm.
Summary: When her mother disappears during a business trip, seventeen-year-old Anne discovers that her family harbors many dark secrets.
ISBN 978-0-385-73559-9 (hardcover) — ISBN 978-0-385-90542-8 (Gibraltar lib. bdg.)
ISBN 978-0-375-89111-3 (e-book)
[1. Secrets—Fiction. 2. Missing persons—Fiction. 3. Friendship—Fiction.
4. Mothers and daughters—Fiction. 5. Grandparents—Fiction.] I. Title.
PZ7.M47844To 2008
[Fic]—dc22
2007041536

ISBN 978-0-385-73557-5 (tr. pbk.)

Printed in the United States of America

10 9 8 7 6 5 4 3

First Trade Paperback Edition

Random House Children's Books supports the First Amendment and celebrates the right to read.

For Libby: daughter,
friend, sage critic

torn to pieces

ONE

ON the far side of Midland Park, which overlooks a field of cornstalk stubble half buried in snow, I lean against a boulder. Its edges jab my back. I wonder if I've misplaced my brain—no, whether I've ever had one.

How could I have been so stupid?

I take the letter from my jacket pocket. It feels crisp in the dark, a little warm from my body. I can't see it. Don't need to. My mind zigzags through every line like a crazy freeway driver.

This is my first letter. Ever. On paper, that is. Everyone e-mails or text messages. Even my grandma Mim, who has no idea how to turn on a computer or cell phone, knows that. But this letter, the one that changes everything? I'm not ready for it.

The wind comes up. I shiver.

Then . . .

Like the far-off rumble of a train before the whistle sounds, a little crack in the wall of my memory threatens to break wide open. I see an image of a snake. Car headlights. A man's creepy face. The words "You'll be sorry, bitch!"

As fast as one picture flies into my mind, I push it away. Take a deep breath.

What do they mean, these fragments that flash too close and terrify me?

I look up. Watch the moon come out from behind thick clouds. Unfolding the letter from my mother, I flip on my pen flashlight. I've read only half of it so far. But I start over again. It can't be true.

Can it?

```
Believe me, Anne. I never meant to
hurt you. You have to understand that
before you read on. . . .
```

"Mom," I whisper, drawing my fingers over each side of the smooth white pages that feel like shark's teeth, "where *are* you?"

TWO

TWO months earlier my life in Centerville had been normal. For me, that is. School, band, best friend, mother, grandparents, black and white cat. Our home, an old two-story of gray stone with a guest cottage, sat back from the road, hidden behind an orchard of crab apple trees. It had probably been an awesome house at one time, but before Mom bought it, no one had lived in it for years.

I tried to talk her out of moving to Centerville. About as pointless as attempting to slow down a tornado. We had already left three cities before that. Every new place was the same: alien faces and classrooms. Lunch alone. Eventually I'd find a friend or two. Then Mom would fold up the tent, and away we'd all go again.

To add to the misery, I was short and fat, freckled, redheaded, and disturbingly shy. Gramps entertained me by teaching me card games and every song he knew. We played chess. After a while I won a few matches. He called me Champ after that.

Sometimes I sat on the porch swing and practiced Beastie Boy, my silver baritone with the dent in the side, until my lips swelled and went numb. Or until Zorro, my cat, started yowling.

Sometimes I read.

Or waited for Mom.

Who was always, always gone.

For the first three years in Centerville, Mim—real name Miriam—and Gramps stayed in the guest cottage but took care of me in the stone house while Mom traveled. But they had always wanted a place of their own. So when I turned fifteen, they bought themselves a small home a block away with pale green siding and black shutters. Gramps grew tomatoes in the back. Mim made raspberry and blackberry jam from the bushes that lined one side of their lot.

The inside I'd describe as having a gray-blue theme with lots and lots of doilies, flowered pillows, curtains. The kitchen, though, had bright yellow wallpaper full of arrogant red and green roosters.

Some say Centerville is the kind of quiet rural town people dream of moving to. Peaceful compared to the city's noisy traffic and living practically on top of your neighbors. Worrying about crime, too. Centerville. Comfortable and familiar, like recognizing almost everyone in town.

Other things make it nice. Enormous trees touching branches over rows of streets that spread out straight and flat as a graph-paper grid. Quiet summer nights except for the sound of crickets. Breezes bringing in the sweet smell of mown hay—a little manure along with it, but you get used to that—weirder yet, even like it sometimes. One mile in any direction and you're on a dirt road pulling up to a barn. To the south, you can sit on the edge of Lake Willow and watch long-legged birds wade in the rushes. To the north is the Centerville mall.

I didn't consciously see the town as this idyllic little refuge from the city. Only a place that I had finally come to think of as my real home.

In Centerville, shopkeepers on Main Street called customers by their first names. Homeowners left their doors unlocked. Everyone trusted each other. That is, except my mother. One of the first things she did when we moved into the stone house was to install an elaborate alarm system.

That should have been the first clue.

But I was only twelve and just a lonely kid in a strange new place.

Until the autumn I turned seventeen, I didn't realize nightmares can visit small towns and the people who live there.

People like me.

I did find a friend. You know how it is. Sometimes people click. Her name was Bianca Colon, Co-*lone*, not the intestinal pronunciation, she was quick to point out. From day one in seventh grade when Bianca, big-boned, skinny, frizzy-haired, said hi with her wider-than-wide grin, she and I clicked. My best friend forever.

Maybe I had come from the city. But I caught on early that new kids in a small town like Centerville stuck out (like me). Some fit in right away. Some didn't (like me). The new and uncool—translation: 1. uncute, 2. unathletic, 3. untrendy, 4. unoutgoing—faded into the cornfields fast. Guess that happens everywhere. Except for the cornfields part.

Bianca Colon was labeled uncool, and she wasn't even new. She was un-Anglo, and smarter than almost everyone. The best thing: She didn't care what anyone thought of her. Period.

Well . . . *almost.*

Her parents immigrated from Mexico before she was born, worked the fields until they had Bianca's brother, Miguel. Then they bought a small produce stand with an American flag hanging above the cash register. Winters they sold salsa and fruit preserves and worked as janitors at the Wal-Mart in Westfield. I loved driving down Route 2 to their old, pale yellow frame farmhouse surrounded by apricot and peach trees and vegetable gardens. Loved listening to Mrs. Colon, the rhythm of her voice. "You come with us for picnic," she'd say. "Is lotta fun. I cook good." In the summer I always went home with a bag of fresh corn or peaches.

It's hard to judge yourself, but I showed signs of being uncool—numbers 1 through 4—early on. Mim always told me, "If you want a friend, Anne, you've got to be a friend." What if I was a friend, got a friend, and lost a friend because Mom decided to say, "Time to hit the road again"? So except for Bianca, I hung back a little. Said no sometimes when I wished I had the guts to say yes, and yes when I should have said no.

Especially when it came to guys.

By ninth grade I had shot up five inches. Thinned down. By tenth, my teeth fit my face. I learned to blot out some of my freckles with makeup. A popular girl said she wished she had eyes like mine.

Cross number 1 off the list.

Maybe.

I noticed guys starting to look at me.

Like Junior Vorhees. Shaved head and pink eyelids. Baggy shorts that hung way down past his underwear line. Drummer in the band with a leg that never stopped jiggling whether he was pounding the snares or not. He let it drop that he thought I was cute, and it got back to me via Lucy Petersen, first chair clarinet. One day by the flagpole he asked me out.

I didn't know what to say.

According to Bianca, self-appointed relationships guru of Lincoln High School, going out with Junior would lead to dates with other guys. If that was what I wanted, and I was a fool not to want it.

I consulted the mirror. What about me interested Junior? Not my freckles or hair.

For sure.

A shape that was okay if not astounding? My personality? Junior didn't know me. He had no idea what I was like.

I had no idea what I was like.

So it had to be sex.

And when it came to Junior and sex, I couldn't imagine us together. I think it was the pink eyelids.

At times, I wished someone other than Bianca, who wasn't exactly experienced herself, would clue me in about guys. Someone like an older sister with answers to my deepest questions. Even my mother would do if I ever saw her. Mim? No way. To her, I was still ten.

Before Junior, I went with Kenny Freitag to an after-football-game dance in the gym decorated with twisted blue and white crepe paper and glitter-covered GO HUSKERS! signs taped to the walls. I was having a decent time until this girl came up to me when Kenny went to the john. "You realize he's trying to make his ex jealous by dating you, don't you?" she asked.

I didn't.

After I said sorry-but-no to Junior, the next thing I knew he and his buddy Wayne Bauer had started rumors about me and Bianca. We ignored them. But one day Junior made kissing noises as Bianca and I walked past. That did it.

Bianca cornered him on the front steps and yelled every profanity she could think of, then started over in Spanish. Junior put his hands on his hips and wiggled them while Wayne laughed like crazy. Crowds gathered, shouted "W-o-o-o-o!" after each insult. With all Junior's gyrating, his shorts came dangerously close to falling down. Lincoln's vice-principal, Mr. Washington, ran out, despite his gross weight problem, and dragged all three into the office. Bianca got detention. Junior and Wayne went to class. I crawled into a hole.

Nobody considered me or Bianca date material after that. One fact about social life in a small town: Kids don't forget. Moving again might not be so bad.

Except . . .

The following September, two new guys showed up, and I changed my mind.

Yet . . .

If I had known what waited around the corner just out of sight, I would have taken off running.

THREE

THE first day of school was warm for September. I walked into the main building after picking up my schedule. Kids stood around in groups on the polished dark gray floor. Freshmen with schedules in hand wandered around lost, looking for room numbers.

Bianca already had left for her first class. If the teacher didn't assign seats, she always chose a desk in front. She liked asking endless questions, which drove other students insane.

Junior and Wayne ambled my way like two hyenas looking for a carcass. Junior's eyes took a tour from my face to my feet. Wayne—he could have been Junior's twin—started with my feet and climbed up. "Loo-king good," Junior said with a whistle, his leg doing its little stutter.

I tried to smile. "So. Ready for another year?"

Junior winked and draped an arm over my shoulder. "Oh yeah. Got calculus fifth hour with Molson?"

I nodded and politely pulled away from him. I made

myself busy reading through my schedule. First hour, band. Then AP History, French III, lunch, AP English, calculus.

"Okay then. See you first hour," Junior said. The two walked off.

I stuffed the schedule in my pants pocket. Glanced around. Waved at two band girls.

In a far corner by the senior lockers, a guy I didn't know, thin with stringy brown hair, leaned against a wall staring at me. At least it seemed that way. The ceiling lights were full of dead bugs no one had cleaned out yet, so it was hard to tell.

I adjusted my backpack and picked up Beastie Boy. Sometimes I wished I played piccolo.

The practice room was across campus over a dirt path past the gym. On the way I stopped and put down my horn. I looked out beyond the school buildings and chain-link fence at the farmlands. Heat rose off the earth in ripples. In the distance an Amtrak train moving north to Chicago looked like a string of glass beads in the sun.

I sighed. Every day for nine whole months in band I'd sit five feet from Junior and his motor foot. In math, too.

Crap.

And then I saw him again, the new guy. In front of me and off to the side, one foot propped up on a skateboard, a little closer than before. Some kids bought recycled stuff from thrift stores and looked okay. His clothes? Wrinkled khaki pants too short for his legs and a rumpled yellow shirt like migrant workers wore—the ones who showed up in the spring in beat-up trucks.

He nodded his head slightly at me.

The weird part: He looked familiar.

John Snyder, one of Lincoln's football players, bumped into him as he passed. "Watch it, jerk," Snyder said.

The new guy stumbled. Kicked his skateboard into the grass. Someone else grabbed it. Threw it against a tree near me.

I waited until they were gone, then picked it up and went over to him. "Here you go," I said. He took it, kept his head down.

"Not all people at Lincoln are mean," I said, my face probably as red as my hair.

When I went to my Jeep at lunch to load my horn in the back, I thought, but wasn't sure, that I saw him for the third time slipping between two cars the next row over. My heart beat a little faster. I locked up and hurried to the cafeteria.

FOUR

HIS name was Evan Jones. Lucy told me when I pointed him out during lunch.

The cafeteria lady and her helpers had hung autumn leaves made out of construction paper above the serving lines. Guys swatted at them as they went through. "Redneck Woman" twanged from the loudspeaker. Lucy mouthed the words and swayed back and forth. I moved with her. We clapped our hands and snapped our fingers. Giggled.

"He's in my third-period art class," she said, nodding her head to the beat.

"Where'd he come from?"

She shrugged. "I don't know. He doesn't talk. He can but he won't."

I already knew the won't part.

Evan sat alone two tables away. He got up, hair falling around his face. I wondered if he had seen me acting like a dork.

The space where he'd been was bare. He hadn't eaten. I could offer to buy him something. Forget it. It would only embarrass him. But he was so thin. Maybe I should introduce myself. "Hi again, I'm Anne." Then what? Why was I even thinking these things?

Bianca, wearing her I'M LOOKING FOR MR. RIGHT NOW T-shirt and skintight jeans, joined us with a mouthful of gossip and two burgers covered with cheese fries. She could eat anything without gaining an ounce.

Evan slipped from my mind.

The other new guy was his opposite.

He had carried his trumpet into the band room that morning, climbed the scratched-up risers with the peeling brown paint, and put his case down on the first chair seat as if he owned it. His hair was long and dark, his face like a model's for a sunglasses ad. Perfect square jaw. Wide eyebrows. He wore faded, ripped jeans and what looked like an undershirt, a tight white one that showed off his muscles. Guys sighed defeat into their tubas. Girls slid headfirst into his blue eyes.

His name was Tal Haynes.

The trumpets and trombones always played off-key and a half measure behind. Tal could read any piece of music without a mistake, first time through.

"Aw, come on, you guys," he said after a bunch of stops and starts, shaking the spit out of his trumpet. "When the baton goes down, it's a signal to blow."

Mrs. Knoepp, the band teacher, tapped her music stand. "Excuse me. Who's the director here?" She soon changed her tune about him. By the end of the week he had turned around the whole section. And wrapped her around his pinkie.

I was hanging on to it, too.

• • •

"You're really good," I told him after the third day of practice.

He had this cocky way of sticking his chin up without talking. Which he did. Then he smiled at me.

I almost ran into the wall.

The second week of school we held a car wash to raise money for new uniforms. Lucy and I polished vehicles. Tal sprayed more water on guys than cars.

"Hey, Anne," he called. We were walking away from the filling station that afternoon. "Can I bum a ride to the bus stop?"

He jogged over and stood in front of us. Squeezed the brim of his faded navy cap and pulled it tight to his head. "Haven't I seen you in a Jeep?"

Lucy pointed south. "She left the yellow monster at school. Want a ride?"

"Sure," he said.

When we pulled into the parking lot, he got out with me. Adrenaline rush!

"I live in Westfield," he said. "Bus doesn't come until five."

I felt scared and brave at the same time. "Would you—do you want to come over for a while?"

"Sounds good."

"My mom's there. But she's actually okay. She's a writer."

"Yeah? And your dad?"

"My dad, uh—" I looked down at my feet. Size nine.

Dad? What dad?

He touched my arm. Voice soft. "Sorry. None of my business."

I walked to the passenger side and unlocked the door. "If you live in Westfield, why do you go to Lincoln?"

Tal cleared his throat. "You don't want to know."

"Oh."

He stood less than a foot away. I always notice eyes. Dark lashes surrounded his, so light blue they were almost transparent.

"Trouble," he said, "with the law. My parents thought a new school would keep me away from certain people, the whole bit." He put both hands in his pockets. "Now that I've told you, are you gonna leave me here?"

Was he joking?

I shook my head. "What are you, on probation or something?"

He smiled. "Yeah, for a DUI. First offense. That's why I take the bus. I wrecked my car. What, you thought I murdered someone?"

My mother met us at the door. "Anne!" she cried as if she hadn't seen me in a month. Actually, it had been almost that long. She turned to Tal, flashed a smile. Made me feel like the most important person in the universe. For a while. "And who is this?"

"Tal, Mom."

"So glad to meet you. Penny Caldwell." She offered her hand. "Come on in. I'll fix you two something."

She wore black jeans and a long-sleeved purple knit top with a white collar. We followed her into the kitchen. From the back, she looked young, especially the way her dark blond hair was piled all absentmindedly on top of her head, an effect that took a long time. I'd watched her do it.

Mom was great around guys like Tal and my teachers and

even the manager of the grocery store. So natural and confident. I admit I was a tiny bit jealous. She could talk to anyone.

I guess a lot of girls would have been happy to see their mothers drop off the planet. Not me. Mom was fun. A little crazy at times. But she didn't bug me or set schedules or preach. She did give me advice about my junior year. "Sweetness," she said, "why don't you get involved in student clubs and make some wonderful new friends?"

Funny thing to say. She didn't have any friends herself. None that I knew of.

The three of us sat on the back patio eating ice cream covered with a blanket of dark chocolate sauce. Mom told Tal when he asked that she traveled, interviewed, wrote for a living, mostly biographies.

I had never gone with her on these trips. Never been invited. The only time I brought up the subject, Mom cupped both hands around my face and asked, "Anne, why sit in a hotel room with nothing to do?" I wanted to say, "I'd love it. We'd be together!" But didn't.

"And you, Tal? What are you doing in the little town of Centerville?" Mom put down her dish, half eaten. She never finished desserts. "Have you been here your whole life?"

Tal leaned forward, elbows on knees. "I'm from down the road—Westfield. Lincoln High—it's all right. I'm liking it so far."

"Tal saved the band," I said, "and we're in English together, too."

"Great!" She looked at her watch. "Well, kids, back to

work. It was wonderful meeting you, Tal. Come again, won't you?"

He stood up. "Thanks, Ms. Caldwell." He and Mom shook hands again. I tried to imagine Junior ever doing that. Or any of the guys I knew.

Later, Tal and I went up to the library. He checked out the two rows of leather-bound Penny Caldwell biographies. I could tell he was impressed as he thumbed through some and looked at the photos.

While I looked at him.

Ohmigod.

Tal adjectives floated in my head on puffy marshmallow clouds: *cute, musical, mature, nice, buff.* . . .

He glanced around the room at the walls lined with filled bookcases. One piece of evidence that Mom didn't plan to move again soon. Like, how could anyone lug away so many books on short notice?

I pointed across the hall at her closed bedroom door. "That's where she writes."

"Is your room up here?"

"Next one down the hall." I was a little embarrassed. It was Saturday: washday. Spread, pillows, dirty sheets sat in a heap on top of the mattress.

I admit my mother had one weird hang-up: She insisted on a clean house. I mean, the whole inside of our place was outdated. Harvest gold, as Mim described the appliances. Dull orange and yellow wallpaper. Brown paneling. Deep, dark brown. Like a mud puddle in the jungle. Olive shag carpeting. Nothing had been changed since we moved in. Not paint, carpet, anything. But each room had to be clean. No, not just clean, fanatically spotless. Sterile. She even kept an inventory of cleaning products with stuck-on labels that said, "Use first," "Use second," "Don't use."

"My mother and I have talked about redoing my room," I said. "That and the rest of the place."

"Yeah, your house, it's really . . . retro. Look at the flowered wallpaper. Like some little hippie sleeps here." He laughed. I laughed.

We walked slowly down the stairs, and at the landing, he said, "I should go. Bus stop is on the next block."

"I could drive you home."

"And show you my dump? Your mom's a professional writer. My dad works at the Westfield lumberyard, and the only things he writes are fractions on two-by-four studs."

"So? I don't care."

Tal looked amused. "What do you care about?"

I blushed. "My family. And honesty. No one ever completely tells the truth—I know that. But what you just said about yourself and your dad? That's honest."

He looked away.

So much for attempting depth of conversation.

I went outside on the porch with him in the fading light of afternoon. The days had turned cool, and I smelled the wet leaves and bark. Crab apples lay all over the yard, too sour to eat. But Mim would send Gramps over soon to gather them for jam.

"Um," I said, "what matters to you?"

"My trumpet. I'm going west after graduation and see if I can hook up with a band." He started down the steps. Then he turned. "Oh, and you."

"Me?"

He paused for a moment on the steps. "You matter." He grinned at me and walked down the driveway to the road. I watched until he disappeared.

I ran upstairs to my room and called Bianca, my heart pounding like one of Junior's drums. "You're not going to believe this."

Before my mother left early the next morning for Miami, she stopped in my room. Her hair was pulled back, captured with a gold barrette at the base of her neck. She wore a black pantsuit over a chartreuse sweater and carried Louis Vuitton, all bought in Chicago. Our house might have been retro, but Centerville did not offer the up-to-date look she wanted when she walked out the door. "Bye, darling. Back Wednesday," she said. "Then we'll talk."

I sat up. "What about?"

"Oh, a certain person's upcoming seventeenth birthday and some other business. Be thinking what wild way we can celebrate. I want it to be extra special for you this year."

"Mom?" I put my legs over the side of the bed. Slid into my slippers. "Did you like him? Tal? I mean, what do you think?"

She sat down next to me. "Hmm." A smile played at the corners of her mouth. "If I were twenty years younger, you'd have a rivalry on your hands. He does seem to like you." She must have read the look in my eyes. "Anne, is this the first boy you've been interested in? You haven't even dated yet, have you?"

"The Hello Football dance with Kenny last year, but that doesn't count."

She shook her head. "You've grown up so fast, and what I—I mean to say is, where have I been?"

I looked down. "You haven't been here. Very much. Sometimes it's like—like you don't really want to be." I raised my head and turned to her. "Do you?"

"Oh, for—" She put her hands on my shoulders. Her face was pinched. "What are you saying, Anne? That I should wait tables here in Centerville so we could be together more? What do you think your checking account would look like then?"

"Mom, I—I'm sorry. I didn't mean . . ."

She rose. Looked at her watch. "Sweetness, my taxi's probably outside. We'll make plans later. Why not invite Tal to your party? It'll be fun." She kissed my cheek. I hugged her. Breathed in her Vera Wang.

"But Mom?"

She stepped away. "What is it?"

"You wouldn't really have to travel. Couldn't you do everything you need to by e-mail? Or phone?"

"That doesn't work for me. I have to *see* my clients. Talk to them in person."

"Oh." I tried to smile, watched her leave my room. Listened as she went downstairs.

The door opened below.

Closed.

And then she was gone.

FIVE

FROM then on, Tal called almost every night. He rode home with me after school some days, and we sat on the porch until his bus came. One weekend we met at Hank's Family Restaurant with some of the band kids. Junior was there, too, but he sat with Lucy and drummed on the table with his fork until she grabbed it out of his hand. Tal leaned back in the booth. Listened. Smiled. A little like Mom. He didn't talk about himself a lot, not even to me. I was too shy to ask much.

I wanted to tell everyone about him, especially Mom, but she was still in Miami.

So I went over to Mim and Gramps's. Actually, I was supposed to stay with them when Mom traveled. She preferred it. So did I. Something about the big stone house at night scared me. But my grandparents cranked up the volume on game shows at their place. The buzzers, dings, "Come on downs" sounded like a video arcade. Gramps also had a job two nights a week phoning the general population of Centerville, asking them to take their recycling to the new plant in Westfield. Most of his calls turned into long, loud "You don't say!" conversations. Gramps was everyone's friend.

So I spent evenings studying at the stone house, which mostly turned into all night. But I had a secret. No one knew about my before-bed ritual. Zorro and I tiptoed into each room and turned on the lights. All of them. All on until morning. Even the one in my bedroom. That way the shifts in the walls and wind moving the shutters and birds and squirrels stirring in the trees, and the werewolves lurking in the dark didn't bother me.

Too much.

Why had Mom picked this house anyway? Maybe it was the guest cottage. She eventually wanted to make it into a hangout for me and my friends (yeah, all my friends). Or the hidden door in the back of her walk-in closet that led to a staircase down to the pantry off the kitchen. She told the three of us about it on the way to Centerville. "I *had* to buy that house! The secret passage is too much! Wait until you see it. We'll have such fun."

Time spent with my mother compared to my grandparents? Who raised me? Mim and Gramps, really. Wherever they were was home to me. I even liked the smell of Mim's detergent better than my mother's. But here's the strange part: I wanted to be with Mom more. She was my idol.

"There's someone new at Lincoln," I told Mim one morning before school.

She paused from her crossword puzzle and raised her eyebrows. "And what is this boy's name?"

• • •

For as long as I could remember, Mim had looked the same. Short. Thin face, squinty eyes, boy-cut, gray-streaked dark hair. Wiry body. She couldn't sit still. Needed to fuss. Mom dragged her into Dottie's once to get her hair styled and makeup done. Bought her new outfits. Mim looked pretty. Two weeks later she went back to her blue knit pants, baggy flowered tops, straight hair.

"I give up," Mom said.

Mim's hands shook a little, so she knitted when she got nervous but tore out stitches and started over. She never finished a cap or scarf but did make patchwork quilts. Lots of them, mostly for children in the hospital. One of the first presents I remember was a pink and blue baby block quilt. I carried it around, probably drooling all over it until it shredded.

When I was thirteen, Mim lost her sense of smell. A frying pan caught fire one day while she had her back to the stove in the guest cottage. Gramps and I, just finished with a chess match, ran over and threw baking soda on it. Afterward Gramps called the incident Mim's "landmark olfactory failure." Her taste buds shut down around the same time.

She thought for sure it meant she was getting Alzheimer's. Every day since, she worked two crosswords and a Jumble. Newspaper looked like a first grader on speed when she finished. But she always finished.

"What's a three-letter word for *ripen*?" she asked, then mumbled, "Oh, I should know that: *age*. I've aged myself, but I'm sure not ripe anymore." She wrote it in. Looked up at me. "Don't get too chummy until you know him better." She put down her pencil. "Edward Healy. I was sixteen, same as you.

23

Sneaky weasel. Took me for a ride on the hay wagon before I had sense to swim away from the boat."

My English teacher, Mr. Harms, would call that a mixed metaphor.

Mim had a sharp edge. If someone crossed her, she bit. That person, five times out of ten, her daughter, Penny Caldwell; three out of ten, Gramps; one out of ten, me. The last one varied depending on who in town currently ticked her off. I remember one fight Mim and Mom had. "Stop dragging Anne all over the country!" Mim yelled. Mom shot back something like, "As if you have anything to say about it." Mim threw up her hands. "To hell with the so-called family lineage. You know she means everything to me." I never quite understood that last comment.

I took my plate and glass to the sink. "His name is Tal." I pulled out my cell and flipped it open. "See?"

Mim squinted.

"Hot, huh?"

"It's the hot ones that can burn you."

"Oh, Mim!" I went to the hallway. "Gramps, I'm leaving."

The bathroom door opened, and Gramps stuck out a round face half full of shaving cream dotted with blood like cinnamon sprinkles on ice cream. My mom had bought him a deluxe Gillette for his birthday. But he still used a blade.

"Bye, Champ. Have a good one." He would, too. I knew where he stored his "little bottles." Here a sip. There a nip. By accident I'd come across a few of his hiding places. He also smoked cigars when he met his friends downtown. Mim couldn't smell that on him either.

She walked me to the door. "When's Penny coming home?"

I shook my head.

"Figures. If your mother isn't there by the time you get back from school, come for dinner. And stay over, too. I'll make the chicken and dumplings you like."

At first Bianca was psyched about Tal and me. But I didn't have much to tell her. I gave him what I thought were appealing looks. After football games I just happened always to end up walking next to him toward the school bus. Wore my warmest smiles. Cutest tops, the clingy ones. Then his visits to my house stopped.

"Give him time," she said. "He obviously likes you or he wouldn't have spent all that time with you. Males operate on weird radar, though. Probably has to do with the moon."

Where did she get this stuff?

But it ended.

Tal stopped walking to classes with me, showing up at Hank's. Calling me. I heard, "My dad needs help this weekend." "Got to run—have a makeup quiz."

Scary excuses like that.

Next week Tal was absent three days in a row. When he came back, he gave me the most pathetic half smile I ever saw and walked in the opposite direction.

"Bianca," I wailed into the phone, "you're not going to believe this."

She already knew. She worked nights at Walden's and twice saw Tal walking by with a big-breasted blonde. When I heard about it, I drove to the mall and tried on a dozen pairs of jeans followed by several pairs of shoes.

You know, to ease my pain.

After Bianca got off work, she and I bought sodas, sat on

the edge of the fountain. She looked at my purchases, asked about borrowing my new pink shirt. Took a drink. Shook the ice in her cup. "Who am I kidding?" she said. "Now, a football jersey—that would fit my big frame. Unfortunately, your pink shirt is made for elves. By the way, Mr. T knows we're friends, but, like, he keeps parading back and forth in front of the store with that female when I'm there."

"I don't care. We didn't quote-unquote date."

"Yeah, well, *date* is an ambiguous term." Bianca pointed. "Uh-oh, speaking of. There they are, the Talsmanian devil and Daisy Mae."

The sight of them was like a rock hitting me in the chest. I couldn't breathe. The two stood close together in front of a jewelry store. Of all places.

Of course I cared. He was so gorgeous!

And we were so over.

That night my mother returned from Miami around two AM. I was still up, trying to finish an essay for history. We always picked our subjects out of a paper bag, and this time mine was the Trail of Tears.

Instead of her usual "darling's," hugs, and kisses, Mom seemed, what was it, worried?

"Got to make a few calls before I go to bed," she said, rolling her suitcase into a corner of her room.

"Right now?"

Mom gave me a weary smile. She took off her jacket. "Unfortunately, yes," she said. "Listen, keep tomorrow night free."

"What are we doing?"

"Tell you later. You need your sleep." She took out her cell phone, opened it, paused. Looked at me.

I got the hint. "Night, Mom."

But after I shut her door, I hung around and listened. The only words I made out were ". . . when did you find out? . . . not enough time . . . that soon? . . . don't know if I can." Another client, another job. I went in my room. Fell into bed. When she was home, sleep always came easier.

Next morning I dragged myself to school. I pulled into the parking lot and closed my eyes. Jerked awake. Stretched. Got out of the Jeep. Put my backpack on the hood while I pulled out Beastie Boy. Could he possibly be gaining weight? Sliding one loop of the backpack over a shoulder, I turned. Evan Jones stood twenty feet from me, his head facing mine over a car.

Okay. Chance to say hi. I'd noticed him on campus, never with anyone. Once I saw a guy knock him out of the way. Evan had backed up against a building and faded into it.

I walked around the car toward him. He was jiggling a piece of wire in the keyhole.

"Hey!" came out before I stopped to think.

Evan turned and looked at me. His mouth trembled. "This is my car," he said. "I locked my keys in it."

"I don't think so. I know who it belongs to."

"You get away. Get the hell out of here." His words ended in a growl.

I couldn't move. He stared at me. I held up a hand. Tried to come up with something to say.

Without another word, he dropped the wire, backed off, turned, and flew through the parking lot on his skateboard.

SIX

THAT night my mother and I went out to a hole-in-the-wall restaurant, Mama Leone's, next to the pickle factory. I knew she had something to tell me because she didn't invite Mim and Gramps. After pigging out on antipasto, we picked at our pasta while some serious recorded tenor sang his heart out.

"Don't want to bore you with finances, but since you'll be seventeen soon, I thought you should see this." She slipped a hand inside her large purse. Out came a legal-size envelope fastened with string twisted around a cardboard circle. "Voilà!"

Mom's face. Perfect with a dash of mischief. Smooth complexion. No freckles. No Botox. Small narrow nose. Straight white teeth except for a tooth on top with a little chip. Her hazel eyes darted around like hummingbirds, but ones behind a screen no one could lift. Sometimes she wore dark glasses. Inside.

• • •

As Mom undid the string, I imagined a wire snake on a spring about to fly forth. Instead, she pulled out several papers and set them in front of me. "Read," she said.

I glanced over the figures twice. "Is it true? Do you have *this* much money?"

"We," she said. "Nothing to be ashamed of. Well, look. I thought about it the other day and decided to show you my holdings and to tell you about your trust fund." Again she reached in her purse for another, smaller envelope. "I do have a will, naturally, but it shouldn't be a secret. Now, this amount will be yours on your twenty-first birthday, and here is the principal, which will earn interest and provide you with enough to make you comfortable." As she talked, she moved a long burgundy fingernail down each column. I felt that same nail down my spine.

"Where—where did you get all of it?" I picked up a half-eaten piece of garlic bread and tapped our current band march on my plate with it. How could ghostwriting pay so well? "What would my father say if he knew about this—this fortune?"

She glared at me as if I'd gone all off. "Father? Listen, Anne. I've told you before, no way on earth could I ever figure out who he is. Doesn't make me look particularly upstanding to admit it, but there you are. Anyway, I invested," she said. "Carefully. Very carefully. At twenty-one you can do whatever you wish with the trust. Spend, save, give it away."

I leaned toward her. "Mom, is something—"

"No, sweetness, of course not. But you're grown up. It's time." She pressed her lips together. "I thought you'd be a bit more . . . pleased. Well. These are your copies. I'll update them as needed." She put the papers carefully back into the envelopes, stacked one on top of the other. "My lawyer has duplicates, so if and when the time comes, contact him. Here's his number."

She handed me a business card. "I've appointed him financial guardian and given him power of attorney if an emergency calls for it." She put one hand against my cheek and held it there. "I said *emergency*. Owen Elling, let's say he seems okay. I hired him when Ira moved to Florida, so he and I only have been doing business for about one year. You're a well-grounded young woman, however, so find someone else if you like."

My toes were cold. "You're scaring me."

"Eh!" She gave me a reassuring smile and took her hand away. "One more thing, Anne." She reached into the pocket of her jacket. "You'll need this." She held out a key. "Safety deposit, First Trust Bank. If something should happen—"

"I knew it! What's going on?"

"Nada. You're my only living relative."

"Mim and Gramps."

"They have their own income. What I said has to do with inheritance. You are my only heir, and you're getting all of it. Is that a problem?"

Maybe. I'd have to think it over.

"What's in the safety-deposit box?"

"Believe me, you're not going to want to run over there tomorrow to find out." She laughed a little, then put her head back and hooted. "The box contains my paid cremation certificate." She pushed the key into my hand. "Deposit it in a *safe* place."

"Oh, Mom! You're only forty-two."

She laughed some more, not able to stop. "I've paid for yours, too. We're both—lying in that—box at the bank. What more could you *ash* for?" She really let loose. High-pitched and squeaky, like a bad clarinet player. That made me start up. The waiter peered over the plastic ivy at us.

I guess anyone's parent could be embarrassing at times.

"Now," my mother said when she had calmed down, "what insane, wonderful thing can we think up for your birthday? I've always wanted to go skydiving. How about it? Or bungee jumping? You, me, Bianca, Tal. What if we all take off at the same time and see who *jumps* the gun by screaming first?"

That got us giggling again. As intelligent and sophisticated as she was, my mother made terrible puns. Just terrible. She knew it, too, but took no steps toward rehab.

As we left the restaurant, I said, "Mom, Tal and I aren't— well, it didn't go anywhere."

"Oh, sweetness, I'm so sorry. He seemed nice."

I sighed. "Yeah. He has a girlfriend. I didn't know."

"That happened to me four or five times at least."

"I want to hear about it!"

She shook her head. "The past is overrated."

Later, I went in to say goodnight. She sat propped up in bed next to the pile of books she constantly devoured and replaced. Once she told me she liked reading a few pages of each first to see if she was a better writer. "Are you?" I asked. "Not in my dreams," she said, "but then, I don't dream anymore."

A ring of light from the lamp above bathed her hair in yellow, her face hidden in shadow.

"I'm glad you're here this weekend," I said. "I hate it when you go away."

"Anne, I'm truly sorry. I wish I could change that."

31

Yeah. If I could believe it. I sat on the edge of her bed. "Mom?"

"What, sweetness?"

"Do you think I could paint my room? You know, get rid of the wallpaper? Every time I wake up, there's this huge orange flower staring at me."

"We'll see. We'd have to strip off the wallpaper first, which takes time."

"I can do it myself. I was thinking of pale blue walls. One yellow one. And a new bedspread—blue, green, and lavender. Splashy. Wouldn't that be cool?" She was staring across the room at nothing. "Mom?"

She didn't answer. I got up.

"I'm sorry. Did you say something?"

I shook my head. "Not really. Oh, guess what? There's this new guy at school."

"Now you're talking!"

I sighed. "It's not like that. He's a loner, and I remember how it feels to be new."

"Of course you do." Her lips turned up in interest. "Life, well, is lonely, sweetness. But you've seen students like him before."

Sure. I was one of them. "The guys at school won't even give him a chance." I picked at the comforter. "He's poor. Wears awful clothes. There's one thing, though."

"What's that?"

"I saw him trying to break into a car at school."

"Oh, now be careful. You don't know him."

"He didn't actually steal anything."

"Because you stopped him. Am I right?"

I nodded.

"What's his name?"

"Evan."

"Evan. Well." She sat up and held out her arms. I collapsed on the bed. Fit myself into them. "You're so good," she murmured. "My compassionate little girl. But don't be naïve. Be a friend to him at school while others are around. Keep your guard up. Always."

"Mom—"

"I've never been more serious."

"Okay."

"Maybe when I'm home for a stretch you can invite him over. We'll see."

We lay like that for several minutes. I was happy.

After a while I said, "I've always wondered. Where did my hair color come from?"

She went silent. "I have no idea," she answered finally.

SEVEN

WHERE, oh where do I begin? You've asked me so many times to tell you about myself, so here goes. Penny Caldwell bares all.

Let me start back in Chicago when I was a young graduate in the early seventies out to write the great American novel. My literary intentions evaporated when I met Teddy Palmer. He wrote, too, but even better than that, he was a hunk. In a few weeks, to help the rent situation, we moved in with this girl I had met at an all-night restaurant over an egg salad sandwich. Sarabande was an exotic dancer who took her clothes off, she said, to Bach tunes set to jazz. At the time I was impressed with the cash she brought home but not enough to try it myself. My legs were too skinny anyway.

Teddy sat on the couch or out on the porch gathering inspiration instead of a paycheck. I finally found a job writing obituaries. I've never told you about my early life, Anne, because I left it behind. Or so I thought.

Then I learned Sarabande and Teddy had been doing their own little private dance routine while I wrote about dead people.

Funny, I don't even remember what he looked like. However, I do recall boarding a bus and crying myself into mush all the way to the Big Apple. After a few jobs—Laundromat clothes folder, deli counter help, delivery girl—and nights at the Y, I begged my way into an editing job with an avant-garde sort of underground publication—very avant-garde, so *avant* I had to be on my *garde* at all times. Ha, ha.

But alone. No one should ever have to feel such loneliness.

EIGHT

TAL walked into English after his three-day absence. He hadn't made it to band that morning. Give it up, I told myself. He's taken. I opened *Madame Bovary* as the bell rang.

Bianca passed me a note.

"Before we discuss the plotline any further," Mr. Harms said, exaggerating every word, "I'd like a few of you to point out examples of figurative language in Part One. I assume you all remember metaphors, similes, and the like?"

Look who's behind you. B.

Mr. Harms's voice disappeared altogether with a *pffft* as if someone had stuffed sponges in my ears. I felt cold all over. Slid the note into my backpack. Began writing my name on the surface of the desk with a fingernail. Down beside my backpack I saw his bare left foot resting on an old sandal, his toes crunched under. It turned his foot into a big dog paw. Joe Anderson, who usually sat there, was absent.

For the rest of the fifty-two minutes, I followed along while Mr. Harms droned on, but when the bell rang, my mind was blank. Except for the image of Tal's toes.

Can you even love a guy's toes?

I thought about him all day. Visualized the two of us together at night. "This is bad," I told Zorro. "Beyond bad." My own cat ignored me.

I had to get over him.

Didn't want to get over him.

Next morning he sat behind me again. Joe had switched to Tal's desk. Tal told Ardis, the girl across from him, that Madame Bovary's husband, Charles, had to be the stupidest character in literature for her to carry on with two men without him catching on.

He had a point.

Toward the end of the hour I felt something touching my hair starting about halfway and moving down. Little shivers covered my scalp. For the first time I turned to look at him. He drew back his hand.

"Hey," he said.

"Hey." My heart was pounding.

"You don't put gunk on your hair. It's soft. So how do you get it all tangled-looking like that?"

"I don't have a choice," I said. "I was born that way."

He stayed behind me for another week. Each time I'd turn to see him grinning at me. Mr. Harms put us in the same study group. We mostly laughed instead of worked. I'd feel something on my hand and look down to see Tal's fingers walking across it.

One day he threw his book in the air. "This is what I think of *Missour* Flaubert's novel," he whispered. It landed on Ardis's head. She screamed, causing Mr. Harms to rise up from his desk like a prairie dog out of a hole. "Sorry, Ardis," Tal said. He turned to me and yawned. "No wonder Emma Bovary hates Yonville. It's just like Centerville."

Friday, when class was over, he brushed my hand with his. Intentional or not, the spark ran right up my arm and almost ignited my hair.

Monday, Mr. Harms woke up and pointed his finger at Tal. "What are you doing in Anderson's seat? Get back where you belong."

"Tal's weird," Bianca said on the way home. "What was the guy trying to prove last week, that he's going into hair-dressing if he doesn't make it in L.A.? I watched him. I mean, he's strange. I don't care if he does look good in shorts and is a genius on the trumpet. No one with half a brain ignores a person one minute and plays with her hair the next."

I smiled.

"Don't tell me you *love* him! Is this the start of one of those grandiose, windswept, bodice-ripping romances?" She gave me a disgusted look. "Why do you have all the fun while I make up romantic stories about myself?"

"I wouldn't exactly call it fun."

More like scary.

"Know what's pathetic? I almost believe them. First, my abduction by a gorgeous highwayman, then the journey through forests and up hills. On the way I dream of what we'll do when we finally stop for the night—"

"Bianca-a-a-ah."

"Don't you want to hear the rest?"

I gave her a look. "Already know it by heart."

We decided to catch a movie. I drove to the dollar theater, where we ate a triple bucketful, the salt from my tears mingling with the popcorn salt stuck to my face.

"Don't know what it was," Bianca said on the way home. "I just didn't feel like crying."

I buttoned the collar of my jacket. "This *is* the third time we've seen it."

"Then why were *you* sniffling all the way through?"

Sometimes you cry at a movie and it doesn't have anything to do with the movie.

Halfway through the week after Mom left for England, I came down with the flu. Mim brought soup and crackers. I was too weak to make it over to her house.

It rained every day, coming down gray and turning the mornings misty. Afternoons went dark early. I huddled under my comforter and had these crazy dreams. Emma Bovary, with all that black hair coiled over her ears, walked through sun-drenched Normandy landscapes, followed sometimes by Tal, sometimes by me asking her for a few love pointers.

The day I went back to school Mr. Harms embarrassed me.

"Now, here's my idea of a *gee*-rate essay," he said, looking my way. His glasses, attached to a black neckband, skidded down his nose, dropped off, and bounced against his green plaid shirt.

I sank in my seat. He shuffled back and forth across the front of the room. Flexed his arms. Rattled the paper. Made a sound like a heralding trumpet to get ready for the reading.

What *is* it with English teachers?

"Of course, you always do well, Ms. Caldwell, but this is exceptional, a masterpiece. It must be heard!" He smoothed what hair he had. Put his glasses back on, took a breath.

I held mine.

" 'Emma Bovary, one of the world's most memorable literary figures and main character of the novel Flaubert set about to write, in his words, "about nothing," stands as the link between the full-blown romanticism of the nineteenth century and the budding realism that would influence all subsequent modern literature.' Now, I ask you, class, is that not a crackerjack thesis statement?"

"Her mother probably wrote it for her."

Mr. Harms looked up and adjusted his glasses with one finger. "Do you have a problem today, Haynes?"

"Who, me? I'm not trying to impress anyone. Sir."

Mr. Harms frowned. Cleared his throat. Resumed walking. Went on reading my paper and finished to polite applause.

By then my face was probably as red as raw meat.

"In his own demented way," Bianca said after class, "T-man wants to be with you. He's holding back, though." She looked me up and down. "However, it doesn't do any good to starve yourself for him."

"I've been sick all week, remember?"

"Oh, yeah."

Tal showed up at my door that afternoon. Books in hand. Smiling. My reaction reminded me of the heroine about to freak upon seeing her long-lost love in one of the Jane Austen novels I had read during the summer. Zorro jumped off a windowsill and ran under the couch with a snarl.

"Your cat always this friendly?" he asked, walking in.

"Only to me. I found him out front starving the first week we moved here."

"And you think he's grateful." Tal put his books on the coffee table. With his muscles, why hadn't he gone out for football? "Anne, I didn't mean what I said today about your essay," he said. "I was trying to get your attention."

My heart thudded. He had it from day one, first moment.

"Didn't mean to give you a hard time." He sat on the couch and put his hands behind his neck. "I said it mostly to bug Harms. So, want to hang out?"

"Um, okay." I felt dizzy.

"Good. Actually, if you help me with something, I'll put our horns together harmoniously. How's that sound?"

"I'm sorry?"

"Your baritone and my trumpet. We could practice. Not that you need much. You're the best baritone player in the band."

I laughed. "I'm the *only* baritone player in the band. But I still don't understand. Why are you here?"

"Why not?"

"I heard that you're dating someone."

For a moment he looked confused. "Oh! You mean Shelley Cook? She's a friend, that's all." He rose from the couch. "I don't take her out, just shoot the bull with her at the mall."

I looked down. Sighed.

"Wait a minute. I'm asking for help with the novel, that's all. The essay coming up? I'm going to flunk it unless the smartest girl in the class gives me a lesson." He grinned and stuck his chin up at the same time.

How could I say no?

"English is my worst subject. Man, oh, man!" He glanced around. "But first, let's get some tunes going."

41

I pointed at the stereo.

"I see it. Are you going to turn it on?"

"Sure." I walked to the bookshelf. Tal, the guy I never thought I'd be with again. Here. In my house. Alone. With me. My heart threatened to fly out of my throat. Confident guys made me unconfident. Guys as good-looking and confident as Tal made everything that came out of my mouth gibberish.

I turned. "Alternative? Metal? Hip-hop? Dance? Baroque? What?"

Tal shrugged. "Your choice."

I slid in Bach's Toccata and Fugue in D Minor and cranked up the volume.

Tal put his hands over his ears. "Hold on a minute. Did I say I wanted to listen to 'Murder in the Cellar'?"

"You said my choice, right?" I felt around for my favorite CD and reloaded the player. "Better?"

Tal walked over. "Much. Now see, when you play something like that, it makes me want to move." He stood perfectly still for at least ten seconds in a *Saturday Night Fever* pose. Then he was hopping, spinning, stomping, grooving, snaking like a crazy on a cheesy reality show. I bent over laughing.

He stopped to catch his breath. Folded his arms across his chest. "Your turn, funny girl. Dance your redheaded heart out."

I couldn't. I went over and fell on the couch holding my sides. Zorro dashed out from under it and flew up the stairs in a frenzy. "See what you started?" I said. "My cat's going to have a nervous breakdown."

Tal walked over and pulled me to my feet. Started up again. I did the best I could. I wasn't a great dancer, but I imitated his steps. We made it across the olive carpet and back nonstop through six or seven songs. I cackled like a laugh track the whole time. Both of us crashed to the floor on our backs afterward. Breathed like hikers on the top of Mount Everest.

That's when my mother came through the front door.

"Well, hello there," she said.

Later, as I tossed a salad and she pulled a pan of chicken from the oven, she gave me her pressed-lip look. "I didn't know you and that boy were seeing each other again. Are you two having sex?"

"*Mom!*"

"You either are or you aren't."

"We were dancing. Messing around, that's all."

"I know girls who messed around and got themselves in a big mess."

I gave her a weak smile. "Shall I pour the iced tea now?"

After that, Tal came by every day. We practiced band pieces. Did English homework. Ate. Danced. Discussed Mr. Harms's neurotic mannerisms, Centerville, my Jeep, the brass section in the band. He went on about everything. Except himself. Or the two of us. But it had to happen sometime. The moment he would move close to me. Take me in his arms.

NINE

I know what you're thinking. Girl with absentee mom meets two new guys at school. Which one will she end up with? Well, you're right . . . *and* you're wrong. But my story also includes another person: my mother. And a letter that tore my life in half. Scary visions from another place and time that crept up on me when I least expected them.

A few days after the incident in the parking lot, I realized Evan was following me. I probably wouldn't have noticed except I was keeping an eye out for him. At lunch in the cafeteria, he sat facing me. Every day between classes, he stood alone with his skateboard near the flagpole. I felt his head turn as I walked by. Once, I could have sworn he stood at the end of our driveway. But I wasn't sure.

Sometimes he ditched classes. Spread out flat under a tree like a tired dog. Tal practiced with the jazz band at noon, meaning he and I didn't ever eat lunch together. So maybe I could start a conversation, hope Evan would answer. But it didn't happen. I couldn't think of anything to say. I was a little afraid.

Then, as I went to my Jeep one afternoon, he materialized next to me like some sort of apparition.

"Are you going to rat me out?" he asked.

I almost dropped my keys. My mouth went dry. "For what?"

"You know. You haven't yet, because nobody's grabbed me. Are you going to?" His voice and breath rose and fell like an old accordion.

"Did you take anything?"

"Did you see me?"

"No."

"Then you can't rat." He turned and walked away across the parking lot. A kind of jaunty walk. Like a person who wants you to think he's got it going. Except he hasn't.

So that was why he had followed me. To see whether I'd turn him in. I slid into my Jeep and sat a moment. Okay. This was it. I patted my backpack to make sure my cell was easy to grab and caught up with him at the exit. "Want a ride home?"

Evan stopped and put his hands on his hips. "Why?"

I couldn't think of a reason.

He kicked at the pavement. "You're probably not going my way."

That's when he looked directly at me. How can I describe his eyes? I hadn't been near enough before to see them. Green, set under straight brown brows. Eyes like dark water found at the base of tree trunks on riverbanks in old paintings. I mean, I didn't even know him, but with eyes like that, he couldn't be unintelligent. Not even close.

Something about his face was out of whack, though. Nose

sort of pointed to the right side of his chin. A decent chin, square–kind of. But both sides around his mouth sank in like a rock star burnout's. His clothes looked like someone tore them into pieces and tried to paste them together again.

I raised my eyebrows.

He shrugged.

Evan climbed in my Jeep and sat with his hands together. I lowered both front-seat windows all the way. He smelled like waxy grease.

As I drove out of the parking lot, he reached into the pocket of his shirt and pulled out a pack of cigarettes. "Nice wheels." He put a cigarette between his lips.

"Where do you live?"

"Know where the viaduct is? My place is underneath. Not really underneath but off to the side. Bet you live in the other part of town. Probably wonder what I'm doing at Lincoln." He lit his cigarette and took a drag. Let smoke dribble out his nostrils. Then chewed on what was left of a fingernail. "I've gone to a lot of schools. They all have different books. It's hard."

"Where are you from?"

"Upstate."

I turned. Saw him staring at me. I looked down. Frayed pant legs, sneakers full of holes. Unlike Tal, Evan had no cool fashion consciousness. But then, neither did I.

"Look, I have a tattoo." He rolled up his sleeve and stuck his forearm in front of me.

"Oh . . . a spider. Wow. Does it symbolize something?"

Evan held up his arm. Rubbed a finger over it. "No, don't think so. Well, maybe."

"When did you get it done?"

"I was pretty young. Probably nine."

"Your parents let you do that?"

"My dad tattooed me. That's what he does. He was going to write my name, but I said, 'What if I want to change it someday?' "

"Good logic. Do I turn here?"

"No, keep going. I did change my name when I was fourteen. My dad never called me anything but shithead anyways, pardon my French. You don't know my name, do you?"

"Sure—I mean, no."

"It's Evan Jones. Used to be Bertie. My ma ran out of names when she got to me. You're Anne . . . whatever. I've seen you around."

"Anne Caldwell." My smile probably looked dry as cardboard. "So, how's everything going? Do you like Lincoln?"

"Hell, no. Like, some dumbass counselor stuck me in the wrong English class, first off. I couldn't figure out what the teacher was talking about. Some dude who went to Africa and saw real heads on poles and the abominable snowman."

"Heart of Darkness," I said. "Not the abominable snowman, though. The main character has a 'fascination of the abomination.' It's an obsession with the dark things people do to each other. I did a book report on it last year."

"Oh-h-h, okay. Guess you're one of those A-plus students."

"Sometimes. Depends."

He pitched his cigarette out the window. Rubbed his nose. "I ended up in brain-dead English. You know, grammar, spelling, learning how to write a check. Why write a check if you don't have money? Over there. That road right there. Take a left."

I saw warehouses. Automotive repair shops. Boarded-up brick buildings. The part of town most people avoided. At the end of the street, the viaduct came into view.

"Right there."

"Where?"

"*There.* You blind or something?"

By squinting, I saw a trailer in the shadow of the bridge. Round, old-fashioned, silver. Except this one didn't have too much shine. Most of it was rusted or camouflaged by dead weeds and tangled bushes on each side. A dented, lopsided blue truck sat in the dirt driveway.

"My dad's here," Evan said. "Guess I can't ask you in."

"That's all right."

"The door's probably locked."

I shrugged.

"No, that's why I can't get in. He locks it when he's there."

I looked at Evan.

"Well, thanks for the ride." He opened the door and stepped into gravel and dry grass. His shoes made a crunching sound. Bending over, he stuck his head in the window. "See you." He stood upright and walked away with a small wave.

"Evan," I called.

He turned. "Yeah?"

"I have this crazy idea you look like someone I might have met before. Have we . . . have we met?"

He shook his head. "Don't think so."

I watched him go up to the door, try it, step back. Glance at me, turn away, disappear around the back of the trailer.

TEN

BIANCA stopped me in the hallway. "Annie, I know you and Tal are together most of the time after school, but I saw something. It wasn't pretty." She fiddled with the frizzy spirals of hair drooping over her forehead. "Something I didn't believe."

Out of the corner of my eye I saw Tal coming toward us. "What, Bianca?"

"Call you tonight." She left, and I watched Tal stroll toward me. All six perfect feet of him. "After school today," he said, "I told one of the guys I'd help him with the tough Dixieland number we're doing at halftime."

I nodded and stared at the face that flipped my insides. Kids looked at us as they passed. I felt proud. "Know what? My birthday's soon."

"Yeah?"

"Mom's planning something special. She said to invite you."

"I'll try to make it. So, shall I come over later this afternoon?"

"Mom and I are cleaning the house today."

"Before the maid shows up?"

"No. Mom thinks—"

"Someone's going to find something murky."

"Quit teasing! She doesn't believe anyone else can do it right. I know. She's weird."

That night Bianca's voice was flat. "He's seeing someone besides you."

I let at least ten horrid seconds pass.

She cleared her throat. "Same bimbo."

"Who told you?" I picked at a hangnail. Zorro jumped up on my lap and purred. As usual, he thought I was talking to him. I scratched around his ears and waited.

"Nobody. I saw them after I left the bookstore. They walked right past me, and I heard him call her Shelley. I know he used to see her, but apparently it's not 'used to' anymore."

I couldn't speak.

"That's my point. He kissed her, too. It lasted twenty seconds. I timed it. And it was deep and messy, if you know what I mean. You deserve more. I don't like popping your love bubble, but if I had a boyfriend who did that to me, I'd say, 'Adios, amigo.' "

When you care about someone, I wanted to tell her, your feelings go all crazy. Especially when you're afraid he might not feel the same. They turn you into someone else. Someone weak you don't respect very much but can't do anything about. "The thing is," I said, "he doesn't act like a boyfriend. I mean, when he comes over he goofs off and sits halfway across the room."

"That's just weird."

Zorro kneaded my arm. I set him on the floor. He walked away after giving me a disappointed meow.

"I even asked him over for my birthday." I got up and walked around my bedroom. "He only said he'd *try* to make it."

Bianca coughed. "You and I have always, you know, done something together on your birthday."

"You're invited, too, ditz. That goes without saying."

"Thanks, but I'm going out of town."

"No you're not."

"I am *now.*"

Next morning after three hours of sleep, I got up. Tal and I? Nothing but study buddies. He and Shelley obviously were . . . I didn't even want to think about it.

Definitions:
Shel*ley *n.* Old girlfriend from Westfield High.
Anne *indefinite article.* Used before words beginning with a vowel sound: *Anne idiot.*

I saw Evan skateboarding along the side of the road and pulled up beside him. He opened the door. "Hi," he said, throwing his board in back. I mumbled hello, spun rubber on the gravel. He took a cigarette from behind his ear. "I'm not feeling that great either. My dad's been acting crazy, so I left last night. Stayed at Schnuck's in the snack bar. Slept there until they closed, then came back at six."

"Where are you going to stay tonight?"

Evan slumped over while he lit up. "Maybe the IGA in Westfield. Open twenty-four hours, from what I hear."

I had driven about half a block. *Oh, great.* I banged the steering wheel with one fist. "You're smoking weed in my Jeep, Evan!"

"Want a hit? Make you calm down." He made a prissy face. "Guess not. Let me out at the corner. I'm not going to school anyways."

I turned right on the next street and stopped in the parking lot of a 7-Eleven. "I'm in an awful mood this morning," I said.

"No shit." He opened the door and scooted the joint under the Jeep. "What's going on?"

I rolled down the windows and fanned the air with my hands. "You're not going to drop out, are you?"

"I hate Lincoln. Bunch of fools." Evan's eyes lowered to his hands. His long, flat fingers pulled at the rips in his jeans. "I'm taking the day off, that's all."

I relaxed a little. "I'm not so fired up about school myself. Not today . . ." I buried my head under my arms against the steering wheel.

"Hey—whoa!" I felt his hand on my shoulder. "Come on, Anne." After a few minutes he said, "You can talk to me. I won't tell. Don't know anyone to tell anyways."

I wiped my eyes and nose on my sleeves. "I have to go home and change this nasty shirt." I thought for a moment, remembered Mom's warning, shrugged. "You might as well come along. Want to?"

Evan shrugged. "Yeah, I guess."

My mother had gone to Chicago for three days to research a meat-packing company and would be back for my birthday. When I walked in the door, though, I had a feeling something had changed. Not the rooms. Not the overall look of the place. Not the smells even. But a sound. Had I heard something? I stopped and tried to think. Maybe it only seemed different because I had Evan with me instead of Tal. I motioned Evan to follow me into the kitchen.

"You guys have a humongous house." Evan walked over to the French doors. "What does your old man do, run a bank?"

I looked away. "I don't have an old man, just an ambitious mother."

"So, your parents are divorced?"

I went to the fridge. Ashamed. The way I always felt when the word *father* came up. "Not many people know. My mother never married. She did everything on her own. Want a sandwich?"

"No thanks." Evan bit a nail. "I didn't know my ma too well. So many of us kids running loose. She died when I was in second grade. Is she nice, your ma?"

"Yeah, kind of like an older sister. She's a lot more fun than I am."

Evan shook his head. "I think you're fun. In a tense kind of way." He looked down. "You don't have to be nice to me. Someone like you. Why would you ever have anything to do with me? No one wants to be with me. Even my old man can't stand my ass."

I didn't know how to tell him I felt alone like him lots of times. The sadness in his face was an echo of the self inside I never showed anyone.

I took a pan out of the oven. "I'll make you breakfast. We'll hang out."

Evan pulled out a kitchen chair. Sat down carefully. "Suppose you won't let me smoke."

"Outside."

"That's fair. Don't have any more anyways. You wouldn't

have a couple I could bum?" He saw my face. "Guess not. I'm not too hungry, but I would . . ." He opened his hands, palms up, then pulled at his shirt. "Do you think I could take a shower or something?"

"Sure."

"I'm really—I know I'm gross. The trailer and everything? No running water for a month. I—you know, get a shower at school sometimes. But last time I went in there Coach Cassidy looked at me and said, 'Boy, you're not in this class. What d'ya think you're doing?' "

"You can use the guest bath. It has lots of towels and soap and stuff and a hair dryer. And a toothbrush. We have a big robe," I told him. "I'll get it, and if you throw your clothes outside the door, I'll wash them while you're in there."

"Oh, no," he said. "Don't touch them, no!"

"But—"

"If you don't mind, I'll wash them myself when I come out."

I tried to keep a smile off my face when he walked in wearing the baby blue robe my mom used sometimes. His hair was glossy. He looked okay. I had set the table and was scrambling eggs.

"I thought you weren't hungry," I said later.

"It was good. Thanks."

My cell rang. "Hey, where were you?" Tal asked. "Nobody knew why you weren't in band. Are you feeling okay?"

"That would be no." I hung up, turned it off. Regretted it. Tal would come over after school. Evan could not be here.

As if he sensed something was up, Evan got dressed and left within the hour. Before he went, he stood by the door and looked at me.

"I'll give you a ride wherever you want to go," I told him.

"No, I'll walk. Want to know something?" He stepped back. "I'm not sure I've ever seen hair as red as yours. Except on one of my sisters."

"You don't have to tell me. It's like a firecracker on a burning barn."

"I was thinking of a maple tree full of way-cool autumn leaves."

I laughed. "Wow, my head is a tree. Mr. Harms would get a kick out of that."

He shrugged. Smiled. Put one hand on the doorknob. "Thanks for the shower and everything."

Tal didn't come over after all. I wandered out on the patio feeling like a dropout. Probably missed note taking in every class, not to mention pop quizzes. Oh, calm down, I told myself. You don't need to worry about things that don't matter when a person like Evan has to spend the night at Schnuck's.

When I went back into the house, I saw the blinking red light on the phone indicating I had two messages. I checked my cell first.

"Hi, sweetness," my mother said. "I won't make it home for your birthday, can you believe? I had to fly somewhere else to finish the interview. The soonest I can leave here is Sunday. What a pain! I'm sure we can have a great birthday celebration next week. Hope you'll forgive me. Sweetie, if you need anything, call your grandparents. I know you have plenty of money, but just in case, look in the bookshelf. I have a little extra stashed there. Bye."

I pushed the button on the answering machine.

"This is Bianca. B-I-A-N-C-A, your loyal friend? What's

55

going on? Why don't you have your cell turned on? Where were you today? Call me."

"Diane? J.J. Contact me ASAP."

Wrong number.

I phoned Bianca.

"I thought maybe that stuff I told you about Tal last night—"

"We're over."

"Sure you are."

"My birthday party's still on, though. Next week because Mom's delayed again. Since we will have it sans Tal, you'll come, won't you?"

"Course."

Before bed I wrote my virtual journal. Had since age twelve. About nothing. Everything. Now: about school, Tal, Mom, Tal, Bianca, Tal, my thoughts on life and the world, Tal. That night I started another section, *E/Jones*. Evan. Different kind of guy. So I'd write about him. Just because. A sentence or two whenever.

The next day Tal called to me in the hallway. I turned away.

Evan stood against a wall as I hurried toward my class.

"Hey, Anne," he said softly. With Tal behind, I couldn't stop.

I gave a secret wave as I went by.

He looked at me the way he did the first day of school.

Out of the corner of my eye I saw him bow his head.

ELEVEN

SO now I'm in New York working for
this rag that calls itself progres-
sive, and I meet a nice guy at a wild
party. He's in publishing, I find out,
as well as into conservatism, so I
don't know why he's there, and I learn
after talking to him for a while that
he's married. That's that, I think.

It didn't end there. We fell in
love. Glorious, mad love with an un-
happy ending, of course. The bad part
is that I didn't get over him for
three years. The good part: a job because of his connection to publishers
and editors.

I had never considered ghostwriting until—I'll call him "Lawrence"—

suggested I write anonymously to get a start since a lot of important people wanted to hire writers to do their memoirs. I could begin with a wealthy member of his extended family, he said.

Anne, I realize I should have told you about my early days of trying to make a buck, but I feared one event revealed would cause you to be curious about another, and before long, as insistent as you are, you'd have the whole sordid story laid out like week-old leftovers.

My three years in New York were fairly innocent, hard, marginally productive. I learned proper social behavior through observation and imitation. My old self, the vulnerable girl with no sense, began to disappear.

Then came the turning point.

I'm such a coward. I can hardly put down the words I know you must read.

For starters, my name isn't Penny Caldwell. I'm just the *ghost* of my former self.

TWELVE

WHEN I drove up to my house after school, Tal was standing outside, arms folded against his chest. All day I had thought about what I'd say if he showed up.

Our time together had been as innocent as a kindergarten class. I didn't know much about him either. Other than the fact that seeing one girl at a time apparently wasn't enough. Problem: My feelings for him couldn't be based on his personality. Diagnosis: Infatuation. Solution: I had to get over him. Analysis: Easy to say if Tal's pretty face wasn't in the room with me.

As soon as I shut the Jeep door, he was standing in front of me. "You hung up on me last night. You wouldn't talk to me today. What's going on?" He touched my arm.

I pulled away and got out my house key.

He followed me to the door. "If I've done something wrong, I apologize."

"I can't sit around and talk today. I've got a lot of homework."

"Could I come in? I'll be quiet."

I had listened with my back to him. I turned. Evan stood at the end of the driveway. What was he doing there?

"I guess," I said to Tal.

Big grin. All over his irresistible face. "Still on for your birthday? What's your mother have in mind?"

"Mom's plans have changed. She won't be back in time," I said as we went in.

"We can celebrate anyway."

"I'd rather not."

The smile disappeared as he walked to the stereo. Flipped it on. Searched until he found something mellow. Turned. "You like honesty? Fair enough. Other girls. That's what this is about, right? Don't know who told you, but I'll bet it was Beeyonkie."

I looked down.

"I thought we were . . ." He put out his hands, palms up. "You're my *friend*."

The first day we were together, he had said to me, "You matter."

What a BSer.

Tal sat on the floor and leaned against the couch. Looked down at his hands. "You know I got a DUI, right?"

"That's what you said."

"Along with my probation, I had to stay away from my buds. That was hard enough. And now I'm in a strange school with no car because I wrecked it." His eyes seemed fastened to the floor. "The only one I see is Shelley when she drives over, and that's not much. She's not my girlfriend. She's my link."

"To Westfield High?"

He nodded and raised his eyes. "That's why I like coming over here. It's nice, comfortable. You're comfortable."

So now I was a pillow. From tree-head to pillow-girl.

I walked to Tal and sat down cross-legged in front of him. "I know what it's like to go to a strange place and miss the people left behind. But you could have plenty of friends here if you wanted to. You're talented and funny and—"

"Nah."

"Yes, you are! All the girls at Lincoln think you're hot."

Tal blushed. I blushed.

For a long time we sat facing each other. I picked at the carpet. Tal looked at the ceiling. Say something, *do* something, I thought.

He stood up. "My bus'll be coming." He went past me to the door. Put his hand up. Looked relieved to be going. "See you tomorrow."

When he closed the door, I walked to the stereo and found the classical station.

Ah, Mozart: So rational. Anne: So stupid.

The doorbell rang.

"He's back!" I whispered as I ran to the peephole.

Evan stood on the other side.

I opened the door. "Hey. What are you doing here?"

He frowned. "Thought you might need a friend."

"I don't know what you saw out there," I said. "I mean, that's . . . private."

"Well, yeah, I understand, but why are you crying? Every time I see you, you're crying."

"I am not." I touched my face. Wet. "Evan, I don't mean to—well, you can't come over here all the time. I have a ton of homework. I missed a lot yesterday." I wiped my face.

"You could be with me. I wouldn't make you cry."

My mouth fell open. "You don't mean . . . you and *me*?"

Evan looked away.

"Oh. That didn't come out right."

"Yeah. Who'd want to hang out with me? But for someone as smart as you, you don't know enough to get rid of people who upset you. Guys you feel sorry for and make friends with one day and blow off the next? That's different."

"You caught me at a bad time."

"You don't know what bad time means. Anyways, it's cool." He turned and did his jaunty walk through the gate.

"Evan?" I called.

He kept walking.

THIRTEEN

FRIDAY, Tal walked off after the football game. I watched him until he disappeared in the darkness. Felt my eyes filling.

Bianca invited me to spend the night. We ate cold pizza. Looked at magazines. Painted our toenails blue. Did our best to keep Miguel out of our hair. He ran into Bianca's bedroom, lowered his Spider-Man pajamas, mooned us, flew out giggling. Later we watched a chick flick. I fell asleep in the middle of it.

Next day at eleven I went home and back to bed.

At four I ate a sandwich and filled Zorro's bowl. I sat down to read awhile. The cat used my chest for a chair until my petting annoyed him and he went off to groom himself. I wondered what time Sunday my mother would come home and went to the phone.

"Mim, has Mom called you?"

"No. Come over. I've made a roast. There's a birthday present here for you from us."

"Thanks, but I'm staying here, okay? I'll study and wait for Mom."

Mim was not happy. But I needed to be alone.

I walked to the floor-to-ceiling bookshelf in the living room and looked at vases, figurines, candles, "objets d'art–fart-aardvark," as my mother called them. Funny, we called it the bookshelf but never put books on it, and the library upstairs, the library. So I knew the money Mom referred to would not be up there. Not that I needed money. In case Evan would talk to me again, maybe I could do something for him—I didn't know what exactly. I turned on KHOP, got some cleaning stuff. Climbed the ladder hauled in from the laundry room. Began on the top shelf. What a dust heap. Mom would freak.

Zorro watched me from his seat on the back of the couch. I looked into, under, in back of each piece of porcelain, glass, sculpture. Wiped as I went. An hour later I reached the bottom right-hand side. Not a cent anywhere.

I sat against the wall. My mother, I thought, likes a joke. She enjoys turning words around.

So what wasn't I getting?

Zorro and I went upstairs, turned on the lights. Went to bed.

In the middle of the night I shot straight up. Had I heard a noise? I usually passed out cold for ten hours on weekends.

Our neighbor's dog barked. Zorro jumped off my bed and ran under it. A slow tingle that began in my toes worked its way up into my stomach. I grabbed my cell and flashlight.

Slipped into each room. Turned off the light. Crept downstairs in the dark.

I looked out the window to the backyard. The moon had created shadows that stretched the bushes and trees across the lawn like a spiderweb. Nothing moved. But a murderer could hide behind any of those trees. I edged over to the front side windows. My heart kerplunked like a messed-up washing machine on an off-kilter spin cycle.

A scraping sound came from the front door. Then scuffling. I heard grunts and footsteps. Close to the door. Across the yard. The phone slid around in my sweaty hand. Should I call 911? We had the best alarm system made. Any attempt to get into the house would call up the cavalry.

The sound of footsteps retreated. The dog barked once. Silence.

I inched over to the door and squinted through the peephole. Nothing. Clear all the way past the crab apple trees to the street. I tried to walk away. My legs buckled. I slid to the floor. Thick lilac bushes sat on either side of the driveway. Maybe someone was hiding behind them.

I managed to crawl to the stairs. Listen for more sounds. All I heard was my own hard breathing and blood whooshing in my ears.

After a long while I went back up to the second floor. Decided to sleep, if I could, in my mother's room close to the hidden staircase.

I turned down the covers, looked over at the clock. Something caught my eye on the spine of a book on the bedside table. The title of the large one under three others: *The Bookshelf: Index to Current Fiction and Nonfiction.*

I pulled out the book. Much lighter than it should be for

its size. Inside was a hollowed-out compartment with thousand-dollar bills stacked in neat, thick, paper-clipped packs of twenty-five. My mouth went dry. How had she saved up so much money? Piles of money! Where had it come from?

A note sat on top:

```
Good girl! If you found this, you can
find more on your way to understanding.
```

Understanding what?

Closing the book, I slipped under the covers, but sleep did not come for a long time.

FOURTEEN

THE person whose name I formerly went by, Anne, was a young woman with a bit of shoplifting experience from her teen days, a girl with a rap sheet of little consequence, really. She paid the price in juvie and earned an expunged record. Even so, when out on her own, she changed her name. Penny Caldwell: innocent sounding, a bright, shiny new penny that would bring much for its investment. Better, don't you think, than a life with parents who would rather have their daughter locked up than at home, freeing them to indulge in the vices they practiced whenever they gave in to them? I had nothing to prove to people who lacked understanding, but everything to prove to myself.

From eighteen to twenty-two, I worked two jobs to put myself through college. Something my detention center counselor said during a session had slipped warily under the locked door of my ear and made permanent residence in the smart section of my brain: "Education is everything. If you want to succeed, you must get an education." She had insisted on journal writing and after a while pulled me aside and told me I might have talent. During my college years I tried to do something about the only compliment I'd ever received. I joined the school newspaper and served as editor my senior year.

Many times I wanted to give up. No one cared, my parents least of all. But I learned discipline while pouring effort and emotion into my studies, hard because of my poor high school habits. Standing alone at my graduation, I cried with relief, vowing someday to rise skyscrapers above my parents and their poverty and never look back.

But what could I do with a degree in English? Speak well? Yes. Write an editorial? Most certainly. Find a job as a writer? Where would I start?

Until I met Teddy, I practiced my skills here and there by designing sandwich boards and new menus for King's Diner during my eleven-to-three job as a waitress, and writing ads in downtime during the four-to-seven shift as cashier at Eastside Dry Cleaners. Even though I *sandwiched* in as many moneymaking opportunities as possible, you could describe this period of my life as a *dry* but *clean* spell.

FIFTEEN

"**HI,** Annie! Happy birthday."

Bianca. I put a foot on the floor and looked around the room. What day was it?

"Did you just wake up? Know what time it is?"

I glanced at the clock. "One?"

"Right. What time should I show up for your party today? You should see what I got you. What's black and white and cold all over?"

"My cat in a snowstorm."

"You sound like your mom."

"Just a minute." I stood and walked with the phone down the hall and into my room, then downstairs. "Mom's not home yet," I said. "I'll have to let you know."

I wanted to tell Bianca about last night. But everything looked normal.

Back in Mom's room I opened *The Bookshelf* again. Real

money, all right. But who made all that noise? I peeled off a thousand-dollar bill and put it in my purse.

I was seventeen today. So what?

I made my mother's bed, my own, fed Zorro. Fixed myself a bowl of Cheerios. While I ate, I read the newspaper and checked the time. Two-thirty. No homework, no mother, no ringing telephone. Mom had a cell but never turned it on. She told me that with all the messages people left her—publishers, clients, agent—the phone would never stop ringing and would interrupt her interviews. She usually gave me the name of her hotel. But sometimes I had no idea what city she had flown to.

Like now.

For the first time, I thought it was strange she didn't tell me. Yes, she usually called to say hi. Mom had a tight schedule. I knew that. Was it my birthday that made me wonder? There were plenty of delays. They had never bothered me before.

Did seventeen make me wiser? Or more suspicious?

For an hour I wrote in my journal. Wrote a sappy breakup song. Figured out the chords. Sang it to Zorro. Cried. Felt better. Worse. I don't know.

Our friendship ends.
We can't be friends
'Cause I love you so much that I cry
Every night, every night
Till the darkness is light,
But we must say good-bye.

So slow, so slow,
You'll leave so slow,

Yet in my heart you will stay, that I know.
Can't you see we can't be
More than friends,
And so, my love, this is where our friendship ends.

At five, I called Bianca and told her to forget the birthday celebration and save my present for later.

She sounded worried. "I can spend the night. Or you can come here for dinner and stay over."

"Your mother doesn't need to see my face again so soon. I think I'll wait here. I'm trying to talk myself out of Tal worship."

"What's happened now?"

I didn't answer her.

"Males! When you want 'em, they don't want you, but if you try to get rid of them, they think you're teasing. They love it."

I sniffed. "I think I might have chased him away."

"I've figured out the male species. Guys know either A, B, or C. I didn't say *are,* I said *know.*"

Bianca and her theories! I went to my dresser for nail polish and a file. Her explanations were not brief.

"Think about it. Males with A knowledge have no clue what makes women tick. Don't know and don't know that they don't know. Your basic loudmouthed, bragging louts."

"Are you making up this stuff?"

"Just listen, Annie. Guys who know B like girls a lot but don't get what they want or need, don't understand about the little things, and therefore stumble around trying to figure everything out until the girls have to tell them, which, of course, we all hate to do or *would* hate to do if we had the chance."

She whispered the next part. "A guy who knows C is dangerous because he understands the female psyche. He not only can give her what she wants and needs but can withhold it at any time and make her suffer. He plays hard to get. She can't figure out what's going on, a serious problem that leads to heartbreak every time."

"Casanova."

"Uh-huh, Don Juan."

I mopped a blob of nail polish off the side of my finger. "I don't think Tal's any of the above. He just doesn't like me that way. Says I'm comfortable."

"What an insult! We need a plan to make him fall at your feet."

The phone dug into my shoulder. I changed ears. "Are you kidding?"

"No. Don't give up, Annie. We'll think of something."

I sat up straight. "Right now Mom's on my mind."

Silence on Bianca's end.

I didn't even know I was going to say it. "She wouldn't have missed my birthday. She never has, no matter where she is. I'm turning into a spaz."

"Wait a minute, Annie. If you *think* something's wrong, it might be. Can you call someone, the police? Have you tried her cell?"

I sighed. "Yes, but she's not calling me back. I'm not ready for the police. I'm going to wait a little longer."

"It's probably nothing, you know? Sure you don't want to come over?"

Truth: I did. But after being with her family, I always realized how disjointed mine was. And it made me sad.

I thought about calling the police, the airport. Watching the news. Instead, I picked up Zorro, my little comfort guy.

We curled up in our favorite chair, the worn leather rocker. I combed his coat while he writhed in pleasure.

But a cat—no matter how cute—can't substitute for a mother.

I closed my eyes.

A car door slamming woke me. A minute later my mom walked through the front door. I jumped up, half awake. Zorro took a flying leap and slid on all four sets of claws down the side of the doorway leading to the kitchen.

"Oh, sweetness," she said, "I'm so sorry. My flight was canceled. I'll make it up to you. We'll have one bang-up birthday next weekend." She pointed. "What's wrong with the cat?"

I burst into tears.

Mom put her arms around me. "You didn't worry about me, did you, my darling?" I nodded. "In heaven's name, why?"

SIXTEEN

AFTER lunch the next day I sat in the library. I put a plus sign on the top left side of a notebook page, a minus on the right.

Plus: No reason to worry. Minus: Worry a little.

Mom

+	–
• *employed in steady career: lots of books to show for it*	• *writers don't stash thousands in hollowed-out books*
• *interviews out of town— but says it's necessary*	• *does not inform me of where-abouts*
• *good mother*	• *never talks about her past*

Should I worry? Mom had apologized, said to quit "fretting." Did I want to know her travel information from now on? Done.

I slid the paper in the back pocket of my notebook. Went

to a computer. Typed in "Penny Caldwell." A lot of publications came up. Some I was familiar with. I read through the list. It went on and on. I closed the window. Then something odd occurred to me. I opened the page again. Looked through fifty references. The most recent one was dated 2000. Nothing after that. Why? Maybe she wrote articles published in company magazines that hadn't made the Internet. Must be it.

Putting my head down on my notebook, I drifted. Thought of my life with Mom, my grandparents, always nearby through all those moves.

Once, we left in a hurry. I was twelve and staying with Mim and Gramps. Mom returned from one of her trips, announced she had found a new place in the middle of Illinois. We'd have to pack immediately because she only had enough time to get us settled before leaving for an extended business trip. She sent me in to empty out my dresser drawers, but I hung around outside the door and listened.

Gramps: "Anne's in for a hard time with another move. You're not home enough, Penny, to see what she goes through. We know what being dragged around does to her."

Mom, très businesslike: "It's something that has to be. I had hard times when I was younger. Much worse than Anne. She's got the two of you, after all."

Mim, barking like a Chihuahua: "I'm getting tired of pulling up stakes myself. Can't you stay put for once?"

Mom, cool as an ice cube: "You committed yourselves. Don't forget the perks."

Then there was that other time, earlier, right after my ninth birthday. Mom and I drove into a gas station. When she came out of the building, I saw a man with a boy at his side walk up to her. They talked just outside the door, the man jabbing his finger at her. She didn't back up. In fact, she stood straight. Said something. Turned abruptly and walked back to the car.

"Who was that, Mommy?" I asked when she returned.

"Just a jerk who thought I took his gas pump." She handed me an ice cream bar.

My head flew up. Like waking from a nightmare. A part of this memory was missing. It had happened before. Each time I saw Mom come back to the car, the scene dissolved. But there was something else. Something . . . terrifying. We had left town in a hurry that same day.

After a while I accepted that moving was my destiny. I was afraid to make friends. Most of the time I did not even have a chance to say good-bye. If Bianca and her big grin hadn't latched on to me in seventh grade, I might not have let anyone get close.

Now. Centerville. My heart grew in this sleepy town. Eighty-year-old brick Lincoln High with the familiar smell of disinfectant in the halls. Warm spring days with the windows open in the classrooms and kids looking out with dreamy faces toward summer. Trucks full of produce at the farmers market waiting for Mim, Gramps, and me. Saturday noons the city hall siren making dogs howl. Every fall our band marching from the school down Main to the football field. Predictable. Easy. I never wanted to leave. Never go back to the city. Never.

I shut the notebook and thought about Evan. Where was he? He hadn't been to school for a week. I hoped he hadn't moved away like I had all those times.

Tuesday morning Mom left again for Detroit. "Here's my hotel, the phone number, my airport info," she said. "See? Be back Thursday." She smiled. "I need to give up this flighty life." She kissed me.

You won't, I thought. "Detroit? Who's there?"

"What do they manufacture near Detroit? Think. I'm doing a history of the typical automotive line worker."

"Oh."

"It's for an anniversary edition of the company magazine. Lovely pay."

Mom didn't need to earn any more money the rest of her life. "I found the cash in the book," I almost said. But didn't.

She paused, looked serious. "Anne? I want you to know something."

I waited. She seemed to be searching for the right words. But instead of talking, she put her arms around me, and we hugged for several seconds until I wondered what was going on. Not that I didn't like it. When she stepped away, I saw tears in her eyes, something she just never let happen.

"I–I– You mean so much to me, Anne. So much." She straightened her jacket, took a deep breath. "Okay. I have to go now. I'll be thinking of you."

"Me too."

After she left, I thought about her words. Wondered why she couldn't say "love."

Tal stood in front of the door into English. I walked around him. Bianca stared from her desk.

"Can we talk?" He looked pathetic. I walked away without answering him, my eyes full of tears.

When I sat down at my desk, I turned to Bianca. "I need chocolate. Buckets."

"You don't have to talk me into it."

• • •

Bianca had struggled to my door that morning carrying a big box wrapped in newspaper.

"For your room," she said, "one thing you don't have."

"Hmm. Black and white and cold all over." I peeled off the wrapping. "Bianca! Cool!" I tore off the box flaps and looked at the minifridge with chocolate chip appliqués.

"I decorated it myself with my sticker maker."

I laughed. "You're crazy. Oh, look, a little freezer section! You spent too much!"

"Don't worry. I got it through my parents' wholesale account."

After school we went to the supermarket, bought whipped cream, cherries, chocolate chips, chocolate fudge sauce, vanilla bean ice cream, nuts, strawberries.

Later Bianca and I lay feet to feet on the couch.

"Chocolate's better than boyfriends," I said, close to sleep.

"You can make a valid comparison. I'm a virgin."

I poked her foot with my big toe. Closed my eyes. "So am I."

Bianca rolled over on her side. "Pathetic, isn't it?"

Mim and Gramps stood outside the door.

"We're here," Gramps said, dragging a big package behind him.

I waved them inside. "Sit down and I'll make some tea."

"No need to fuss, Champ." Gramps pointed to my gift. "I'll take the paper with me. It's the recyclable kind."

Mim walked to the couch. "Mom home yet?"

"Yeah, but she left. Detroit."

"Gone again, huh?" Gramps set the present in front of me. "You'll like this."

Mim looked either worn-out or really old. I hugged her first, then Gramps. "Open it now," she said. "Your other present is in the works."

"A quilt, right? You've already made two for me."

Gramps pointed. "Go ahead. Tear."

"Hmm, what's in here?" I pulled the paper off the larger one. "A suitcase?" I stood up. "Is this the way I'm finding out? Is that what my mother is doing right now, looking for a new home?"

"Hold on!" Gramps said. "Penny suggested the luggage, but she didn't mention moving, only that you'll need it for college."

I felt sick. "I don't believe it."

"Champ, we're not going anywhere." Gramps pulled out a handkerchief and wiped his forehead. Under his breath he said, "Better not be!"

I didn't buy a word of it.

Next morning, I stopped at home. Zorro dashed out the door as I entered, probably to mutilate some bird he'd seen from the window. He'd been spending a few nights outside lately.

I picked up my backpack, change of clothes. Saw one phone message blinking. I pushed the Play button.

The voice was low and deliberate. Threatening.

"Diane, I told you to call. Get off your ass. *Now.*"

Diane?

I erased the message and went to school.

I decided to spend another night at Mim's. When we finished putting away the dishes, the three of us ate popcorn and played Aggravation until Gramps fell asleep in the middle of a move. Next day after school, I drove right to the stone house to see if Mom had come back.

The phone wasn't blinking. Mom hadn't called my cell either, meaning she might be on her way.

I went into the kitchen to scrounge some food. Found an apple in the fruit bin. The weather was warm. I went out to sit in the sun. Just as I closed my eyes and leaned back in the lawn chair, I heard a rustle, then a snap, coming from the far side of the yard near the guest cottage bordered by a row of elm trees. I jumped up. Wondered when I'd get smart and take my cell everywhere.

I backed up toward the door. The slightest sound of crunching leaves sent my heart skyward. From behind the trees, someone got up and started toward me. It couldn't be.

He had Zorro in his arms. Zorro never let *anyone* but me touch him.

"Evan!" I whispered.

"S'up?"

SEVENTEEN

"I'VE been crashing in your yard a few nights," he said after we went inside. He scarfed down three grilled cheese sandwiches and drank at least a half gallon of milk. "Pretty comfortable, actually. I scooped up a pile of leaves to sleep on. Where you been?"

"When my mother's out of town I stay with my grandparents right down the street sometimes. How about you?"

"Around. Nowhere. Trying to figure out what to do. It's nothing that hasn't happened before."

"Where's your dad? Has he left Centerville?"

"Maybe. I haven't been back to the trailer. More peaceful in backyards." He stretched and got up. "You're the only one who hasn't treated me like trash. So that's why..." He smiled and shrugged. "I'd better go. I won't show up anymore and scare you to death."

"How did you get Zorro to come to you?" I asked. "He

won't even let my best friend touch him. And he's really afraid of guys."

"I woke up with him next to me this morning."

As if I weren't there, Zorro walked by me and hopped on Evan's lap.

"Zorro's a good cat, aren't you, boy?" Evan scratched my cat's ear. Petted him. Zorro squeezed his eyes shut. A sign of respect. Evan put him down carefully. "I'm gonna get going."

"Wait. Let me ask you something," I said. "Were you here last Saturday night, late, in the front near the door? I heard a scraping noise."

Evan shook his head. "I've only been out back for three nights. Must be since Monday, right? So it wasn't me."

I put away the food and washed the frying pan. "You can't live outside. What happens when it really gets cold?"

"Haven't thought about it."

I pointed out the window. "You could stay there." Evan gave me an are-you-out-of-your-mind look. "No, really, we have plenty of room. If you want, you can help us out with yard work, something like that. But look, the guest cottage has a bath and kitchen. My grandparents lived there for a while. We never use it, so it'll have to be cleaned up, but it's better than the yard. What do you think?"

He didn't answer.

"You need a place to live, right? Free rent. You also could keep an eye out, tell me if anyone's been around."

"I don't think–"

"And ride to school with me every day."

He looked out at the guest cottage. "You don't have to be nice. Anyways, I don't know if I can do school."

"It would be good to have some company."

83

"Yeah, as long as it's not me."

"Come on! Know what? There'll be a place here for you to sit and study. Nice and quiet. It's worth a try, right? If you need to catch up, I'll help. With English, at least. My friend Bianca is a total math genius. She explains stuff to me all the time. How's your math?"

"Gives me a gigantic headache." Evan sat down again and groaned. "I don't know. I'm a wrecked car. I don't have any idea where to start pounding out the dents. For sure, my ignition is shot."

But he wouldn't stay. No matter what I said.

I didn't see him at school Tuesday. No word from my mother that day or the next. I avoided talking to Tal. Bianca went to work. I sat on the front porch and thought about Mom. How she couldn't possibly care. Because if she did, she would have called me.

Mim arrived on foot about four, holding a newspaper over her head. It had started to rain. "I've come to get you for supper," she said. "You're not eating right."

"Love your cooking," I told her. "It's just that I want to stay here and wait for Mom, okay?"

"Mom, shmom."

"Come on, Mim." I picked up an umbrella inside the door and walked her to her house, holding her hand the whole way, hoping her feelings weren't hurt.

As I turned around and started back up our driveway, I blinked. Evan sat on the porch steps. I waved.

He didn't move.

"Evan?"

As I got closer, my heart sank. He had a black eye and a

swollen lip. The left side of his face was cut. Rain had soaked through his shirt and turned his hair to strings.

"What happened?" I dropped the umbrella and sat next to him, touched his face, then pulled back my fingers when he winced. "Did some idiots from Lincoln ambush you?"

He wouldn't answer. But when he tried to stand, he stumbled, and I had to hold him up.

"Are you sick?"

He coughed. "No."

I took him into the kitchen and wiped his wounds with alcohol and antiseptic. Evan was silent the whole time. I filled a plastic bag with ice cubes. He held it to his eye and face.

"I'm so tired," he said. His good eye was gray.

I fixed a can of chicken soup and watched him try to get it past his split lip. He put his head down on the table afterward and fell asleep. For a while I sat beside him and wondered what to do. Then I tapped his shoulder. He rose up and looked around as if he forgot where he was.

"How are you feeling?" I asked.

He put his head on my shoulder.

"Come on," I said. "You can sleep out in the guest cottage tonight. Don't worry. I won't make you stay."

Without a word, Evan got up. I held on to his arm and steered him across the lawn. Inside the cottage, I found some sheets and a blanket, went into the small bedroom, and spread everything over the bed. Evan lay down right away and turned toward the wall.

I put the blanket over him. "Talk to you tomorrow," I said.

He was already asleep.

Next morning I checked on him. He was sprawled on his back, still out. His face had to heal before he could go to school again. It looked awful. I left sandwich meat in the kitchenette fridge, bread and a note on the table telling Evan to eat.

When I drove up at three-thirty, he was sitting on the porch again. As soon as I closed the door of my Jeep, he stood. His voice was hoarse. "I know what I said. But your offer about the house out back. If it's still okay?"

"Of course," I said.

"You need some new clothes," I told him later.

"Yeah, for about my whole life."

"We'll go shopping tonight."

"Huh? No."

"Okay. I don't have much common sense, but I do have the kind of *cents* found in a wallet."

Great. I really did sound like Mom.

Evan folded his arms across his chest. "I won't owe anyone. That's my rule."

"Come on, then. We'll ride around for a while."

I drove to a mall three towns away. No use running into someone from Lincoln. On the road, I tried to convince him about the clothes. No go. Finally I said, "Think of it as a loan. Someday, you can pay me back. But you need clothes now. Tell me I'm wrong."

We ate a burger and milk shake in the food court. Afterward, we hit the department store. Evan picked out jeans, shirts, shoes, socks, and underwear.

"Is this too expensive?" he asked.

"No."

"What about this?"

"No. And leave your old clothes in the dressing room."

"Why?"

"Are you kidding?"

"Yeah."

I gave him money to pay so that he wouldn't feel funny.

After some persuading, he followed me into a unisex hair salon. "What do I do?" he whispered.

"Just tell whoever to give you the cut all the guys want," I said, "unless it's a shaved head."

I looked him over as we walked out. "You look good." Except for his cheek, which had turned a nice greenish yellow.

"I'll have to trim your trees and paint the house to pay for all this." He lifted up one of his feet to check out his sneakers and smoothed his shirt. He smiled at me. Gave me an awkward hug. Then laughed and split open his lip again.

I'd have to tell her about Evan, but Mom would go along with it. I knew she would.

My mother! It was eight o'clock. Maybe . . .

"We need to get going," I said.

I called to her as we entered the house, but could tell she hadn't come home. Evan and I gathered up his packages and clean sheets and towels and went out to the guest cottage. Not much furniture, but enough. The former owner sure liked turquoise appliances, brown floor tile, and good old olive carpeting. I slid open the windows to get rid of the stuffiness. Evan walked around the three small rooms.

"A bed, a nightstand, couch, kitchen, bathroom—a lot bigger than the trailer," he said. "Are you sure about this?"

"Um-hmm. See you in the morning. Are you ready to go back to Lincoln?"

He touched a hand to his eye. "I'm ready for a hot shower," he said.

I took that as a no.

I waited up until midnight. Next morning, Mom still hadn't come home. I went to the Jeep. Evan was standing next to it. Except for his eye, he looked like a regular Lincoln High student in jeans and a blue shirt.

"Where'd your skateboard go?" I asked on the way.

"Broken. Some guy." He looked out the window. "There's going to be too much makeup work."

I drove into the parking lot. "Don't worry about it now."

"Here, I'll carry your case." He pulled Beastie Boy out of the back of the Jeep.

I saw Junior and Wayne watching us.

"What are you doing with a loser like that?" Junior said. He walked in front of my Jeep.

"Ignore him," I told Evan. "Come on." I pointed in the other direction.

"Hey, look at you. All decked out. Anne get you those, loser?"

"Cut it out, Junior. Faster," I said out of the side of my mouth.

Then the two of them were next to us. "How sweet. Annie has a boyfriend."

Evan stopped and put down the horn.

"Don't," I told him with my head down. "Keep walking."

Just like that, Junior grabbed Evan by the arm and punched him. He fell over my horn case and landed on his back in the middle of the parking lot. He wiped his nose. Blood stained his new shirt.

Junior pumped his foot up and down, then swung his

boot back to kick Evan. As hard as I could I shoved him sideways. He slammed into a car. His shins hit the bumper, and he went down.

"Dude, she burned you!" Wayne stood wide-eyed while Junior pulled himself up. Evan sat and rubbed his elbow. Kids gathered.

"What are you doing with that guy anyway?" Junior asked me. "You're going to be sorry."

"I already am. Sorry I ever met *you*."

"Burn two!" Wayne doubled over. "Give it up, Junior! She's smarter than you."

"Shut up, Bauer."

I saw Tal walking toward us. Where had he come from?

He pointed at Junior. "Hey, drummer boy, what's going on?"

"Nothin'."

Tal smiled. Not like any smile I'd seen from him. It wasn't friendly. "Move it," he said. "Stay away from Anne."

Junior limped past me. "Jerk," he said under his breath.

Tal folded his arms against his chest. "Don't go near her again."

Wayne gestured with his head toward me. "That girl don't need protection one bit." The two went off, Wayne still laughing.

Tal came over, put his hand on my shoulder. "He ever messes with you, tell me. Promise." I nodded. "Good. See you in band."

My heart pounding, I watched him walk off, then turned to say something to Evan. He was gone. Along with my baritone.

When I reached the band room, it was sitting next to my music stand and chair.

EIGHTEEN

"**YOU** should come up with a pen name," a friend suggested, "for your biographies. If you want to use your real name for other writing, you won't be categorized."

I had already been using "Penny" for several years and said I didn't have time to write high-quality fiction, if that's what she was referring to. I certainly didn't divulge to her that one of my clients had proposed an activity with financial returns far beyond my ghostwriting income. At first, I merely laughed at him and asked what made him think I'd do anything like that. But at home I added up my earnings over the past several months, so *paltry* it was ap*palling*, then compared this with figures from my client. There was no comparison. However, I didn't act on the opportunity for almost a year after you, my precious, came into my life.

I guess I now must let another of those rambunctious cats out of the bag, and I don't mean Zorro, our sweet little bandit with the mask and cape. I know you think I had an affair, became pregnant, had you, and kept you after your father left. Of course, the first part is true. I've had more than one affair, though most of them were anything but *fair*. The story of your birth is much more complicated than simply passing on information. In fact, the whole thing should be featured in *Ripley's Believe It or Not*. Consequently, you may *believe* what I'm about to tell you, but you're *not* going to like it.

NINETEEN

MY mother didn't come home. Or call. I tried not to worry. Okay, I was freaked. Something was beyond wrong. I had to find out what. But how? My grandparents didn't know anything.

After school Friday I told Mrs. Knoepp I couldn't play at the football game that night. Then I met Evan. "Know how to drive a stick shift?" I asked.

"Yeah. Never got a license."

"That's okay."

He wasn't bad. A little fast around the corners.

He turned into the driveway. "Your ma's not back yet?"

"No. Macaroni and cheese—you like that?"

"Sure. Want me to help?"

"You can cook?"

"Not really. I could try."

"I'll order us a pizza. Okay if we eat in about an hour?"

"I'll work on the little house. I'm moving around some of the furniture. Is that cool?"

I smiled. "Very cool."

Inside I lowered my backpack to the couch. Where had I put the number for my mother's hotel in Detroit? It finally showed up under a pile of papers on my desk. I dialed and waited. When a man answered, I gave him her name and asked him to ring her room. After a minute, he took me off hold and said, "We have no one by that name at this hotel, but there's another Hyatt at the airport. Would you like me to call someone there?"

I said I would.

"According to our computer," the man told me a few minutes later, "Penny Caldwell has not registered here or at the airport Hyatt within the last thirty days."

I thanked him and hung up. Next, I called Mom's cell. "The number you have dialed has been disconnected," the voice said.

I felt a catch in my throat, panic tingling in my chest.

"Mim, are you sure she hasn't called?"

"She left you the wrong hotel number? That's odd. Have you tried some of the others?"

"How many hotels would I have to call in Detroit?" I was close to tears. "Besides, I'll bet she didn't go there at all." I twisted one of my millions of hair strands around a finger. "Do you know something you aren't telling me?"

Mim paused. One of those nanoseconds that say *yes*. "No," she said. "I was just trying to decide if Penny said Detroit was on her itinerary this month."

Mim, get off! I thought. What itinerary? Most of my mother's trips were not planned. She took assignments whenever they came. We all knew that.

But Mim didn't sound worried. Was I acting crazy? I

thought of Mom's phone conversation the night she came home late and I listened outside her bedroom door.

". . . not enough time . . . that soon? . . . don't know if I can."

Now it sounded important.

Within ten minutes, Tal walked up the driveway. "I heard from Lucy you aren't marching tonight," he said as I opened the door. "Something wrong?" He walked in past me. "Where's your mom?"

I stepped in front of him. "My mother's late, really late, coming back from a trip. It worries me."

"Where did she go?"

"Detroit, but I haven't been able to reach her."

He thought for a moment, then said, "So, do you believe her?"

"Why wouldn't I? She's traveled like this practically my whole life."

"Anne," he said, "excuse me for saying it, but someone who's really on the job isn't going to have this kind of schedule."

How could he say that?

Even if it might be true?

"She writes about people," I said. "People all over the world. And businesses. I have no idea how many. She doesn't have a boss. She works alone. I mean, maybe she's not as normal as your mother, but that's what my mom does, and it's normal to me."

"But you still don't know where she is." He took a deep breath and glanced around the room. "I'm sorry about all of this."

"Thanks."

He relaxed a little. "So. About your birthday. I can barbecue and make us salad."

I shook my head. "You shouldn't really be here."

"How about a lazy Saturday tomorrow? I'll call in the morning. Maybe you could come to my house for lunch. My parents would like to meet you."

Why would Tal want to introduce Anne the Pillow to his parents? Did he feel something for me? Or was he yanking me around? I bit my lip.

"Has that skinhead bothered you any more?"

"Junior? No." I walked across the room. "What bothers me is Mom." I wanted to tell him how scared I was. My worry of possibly having to move again. Or to call the police.

The phone rang.

"That you, Diane?" Same low voice.

"No," I said, "you have the wrong number."

"Is this the daughter?"

"Please check the directory if you're looking for Diane—whatever her last name is."

"Stillman. Diane Stillman. She needs to call J.J." He hung up.

I turned to Tal. "Some guy named J.J. is looking for Diane Stillman. This is the third time he's called."

Tal shrugged. "The world is full of loony tunes and wrong numbers," he said. "About tomorrow. Why don't you drive down at eleven?"

The doorbell rang. Tal strolled to the door and opened it. Bianca stood outside in a sweatsuit with a laundry bag over her shoulder. "Sri Lanka Bianca," he said, grinning.

"Tal-butt." She pushed by him. Left the door wide open. Came over to me. "My dad dropped me off. I'm staying with you tonight, and don't say no. You need me." Under her breath she said, "Why is *he* here?"

Then Evan stuck his head and shoulders in the door. "Anne?"

"Who are you?" Tal asked. "Wait. You go to Lincoln."

Bianca raised her eyebrows.

Evan glanced at both of them and shrugged. "I do the yard." He turned to me. "What part today? Front or back?"

Tal looked out the door past him. "Where's your truck and tools?"

I wiped my hands on my shorts, felt like a bird caught in the crosswinds. "We have a mower and a weed eater." I looked at Evan. "Actually, it's getting late, so can you come back next week?"

"Not a problem." Evan shut the door behind him.

Bianca cocked her head. "I remember. He's the one with the moldy skateboard. How come you know him?"

Translation: "Why haven't you told *me* you know him?"

"We started talking one day. He said he could use work."

"Yeah, he needs something, all right. But your grandpa does the yard work."

The girl could really dig for information.

Tal looked annoyed. "Gotta catch the bus," he said. "Tomorrow, Anne."

As soon as he was gone, Bianca said, "Back again, huh? I'm right. Tal knows C. No doubt in my mind. He's into torture. But what's up with this other guy?"

"Let's micro some cheese crisps, and the three of us can get better acquainted."

"What three? Does Zorro eat cheese?"

"Very funny. Evan. He's living in the guest cottage."

Bianca dropped her laundry bag. "No way! How did that happen?"

So I told her, and when we had our snack ready and I went to get Evan, he was gone, and the little place was dark.

That night my mother still did not come home.

Saturday, I actually went to Westfield. Tal's mom and dad, both young-looking, welcomed me like a favorite relative. His dad had on jeans and a dark blue golf shirt, and his mom wore cargo pants with a long-sleeved white sweater. They weren't much like the parents at Lincoln who came to the football games and band concerts. These two did not carry an extra ounce of fat. Probably why Tal was so fit.

The house, kind of bare, reminded me of motels we had stopped at in the past. With furniture so plain it's indescribable. I saw a picture on the living room wall of peach sailboats on gray water. Another of a fluffy dog sticking its nose in a watering can. But no knickknacks like the ones at Mim's. Not an object anywhere. Not a book. Just a few magazines, the ones you get free at the grocery store. And Tal's parents, they seemed to be trying really hard.

All during lunch Mr. Haynes teased Tal about his long hair. Called him Sonny. Said Sonny this and Sonny that. His mom cracked up the whole time. I laughed because she laughed. Once, when Tal's dad reached for the salad, I noticed his hands. Smooth and slender. I never could have guessed that he sold lumber.

Afterward, Tal took me outside. "Close your eyes," he said, then put a gold chain with a single pearl around my neck. "Happy birthday, Anne."

How could Tal afford it? He didn't work, and his parents didn't seem to have anything. Embarrassed, I raised my eyes to his face and saw an expression that confused me. Kind of like Gramps's when I fell off my two-wheeler at six and cut my knee. Sympathetic. Why would he feel sorry for *me*?

I wanted him to kiss me. So much. Isn't that what guys do to birthday girls? But he stepped away. "Let's take a ride," he said. "We have a couple of old bikes hanging up in the garage. Go in and find us some cold bottles of water."

Before I left, I got out my cell and asked Tal's mom to take our picture. "I want to see big smiles from both of you," she said, laughing again.

Late afternoon I walked to the guest cottage. Evan hadn't shown up at all the night before. The lights had still been off when I went to bed. I knocked, tried the door. The smell inside was strong.

"Hey, Evan," I called, "you awake?"

I heard rustling in the other room. He came out wearing a pair of jeans, no shirt, looking sleepy.

I got right to the point. "Please don't do drugs here. My mom wouldn't object to your staying with us. But weed? Not a chance." I pulled out a chair and sat. "If you have to smoke cigarettes, that's your choice."

Evan blinked. He went into his bedroom and came back with a shirt on.

"Are you okay with that?" What more could I add without sounding like Mim?

"Fine," Evan said, yawning. "Whether I can promise? When I go out, I don't have plans to—to get high. But if someone offers me shit, I take it. See what I'm saying?"

It was like that with me and chocolate, but I didn't think it was quite the same. "Who's giving it to you?"

He didn't answer.

I got up and went to the door.

"Did you like the bit about the yard guy? You were with that dude again today. Looks like you two are getting along now." He coughed up something and went to the sink. "Oh yeah, thanks for the food in the fridge."

"I thought it would be easier for us if you—"

"Stayed away from the house."

"No, that's not why. I don't want you to go hungry. It wouldn't kill you to gain a few pounds." I walked back. "So, do you want to talk?"

He stood, quiet for a while, and looked out the window. "I wish I had something interesting to say, you know?"

I smiled. "Come on, Evan. Tell me stuff about where you used to live. Your family."

"No, not that." He shook his head. "I was thinking. Living here is so—so *cool* compared to being with my old man. I have no clue where he is these days. Don't get me wrong. I don't want to know."

"I'm glad you're here," I told him.

In bed that night I wondered how I felt about Evan. He had a home. For now. How long, I didn't know. But I wanted him to stay.

Tal. I had to do something to kick-start his interest in me again or I'd go crazy.

My thoughts drifted. A memory nagged at the outer edge of my mind like an ache. Right before she went to Detroit, when Mom hugged me and said I meant so much to her, she had almost cried. Was she saying good-bye to me that morning the only way she knew how? Was that what it was? I lay there for a long time wondering.

As I floated toward sleep, a little voice that sounded like my own whispered, "Yes. That's it exactly. Now she's gone. Penny Caldwell is gone. This time she's not coming back."

TWENTY

I was living alone in Chicago the year you were born, having forgotten all about Teddy and Sarabande and Mr. New York Wonderful. I had moved way beyond that early experience.

Again, when I didn't have an assignment, I sat at my typewriter and worked on the novel I knew would get rid of the "with" before my name. If a publisher accepted it, I decided, I'd use my real name. Assigned biographies took organization, not talent. But fiction. Would I get anywhere? My life sat as still as a pond in August.

As the old saying goes, "Truth is stranger than . . ." You know the rest. In my case, Ruth and what followed were crazier than fiction. I didn't even know her last name, but she came to one of the get-togethers I threw to have a few people around, and soon we were roommates. I had vowed never to live with anyone else again, but Ruth had a job downtown with one of the top law firms and paid her part of the rent in cash. She told me she'd stay five months until her transfer to L.A. I couldn't pass on her offer. I'd really never had any extra money, and because of her, I put away a little.

Ruth decided to stay longer, and I knew immediately it was about a man who wouldn't be going to the coast with her. I observed first, as the weeks passed, the pasty pancake color on Ruth's skin replaced by a healthy glow, the slight protrusion of her belly, her happiness, then sorrow. Finally she told me, "Penny, he's married and going to stay that way. I need to get rid of it."

"Don't do that!" I yelled, surprising myself. "Don't you dare even think of doing that!"

I had always dreamed, in my weaker moments of femininity, of having a baby, of how good it would be to love and take care of my own child. We talked adoption, and she finally agreed it was the best option. But then, just as she decided to allow her baby to have life, she found out she, in fact, was not long for this world. The irony of it. Life and death and me in the middle.

TWENTY-ONE

SUNDAY, Evan and I sat around in the kitchen over coffee and bagels most of the morning. I told him I had known Bianca since seventh grade when she asked how she could get her hair to turn orange like mine. Evan said his friends were the old men on the street near his dad's shop. Sometimes he'd get a quarter from one of them. Most of the time he held out the sign A-1 TATTOOS or showed off his spider. Or encouraged bikers to go in and see all of the designs.

"What were you looking for when you tried to break into the car?"

"Oh, that." He kept his eyes on the cup he moved around in little circles. "I was pretty desperate for something I could make money off of. There was a CD player on the seat and a camera if I got the door open. You scared me so bad when you yelled at me that I never did give it another try."

"Yelled at you? I didn't really, did I?"

"Yeah, well, it's a matter of—what do you call it?"

"Semantics?"

"I guess. Anyways, I wonder what would have happened if you hadn't helped me. I don't know where I'd be. Probably in jail."

In the afternoon we went out to work on the yard. My mother had let it go the first couple of years until Mim told her the place was ratty. Gramps usually took care of the mowing, trimming, and gardening, and I had helped. What we planted produced different flowers all spring and summer. I figured working in the garden would give Evan and me something to do together. Take my mind off Mom.

The weather was turning cold again. I pruned the mums, separated the iris bulbs, put them in bags for the cellar. Next I planted the tulips. Evan helped rake several basketsful of leaves. Put them in trash bags. Later I made us hot cocoa. It was bitter, so I added a lot of sugar.

"Let me get something," he said. "Be right back."

He carried in a section of a cardboard box and a piece of heavy paper. "Put your hands on the table," he said. "There. Now sit up and look out the French doors."

"You're going to draw me!" I said. "No one's done that before."

"I designed some of the tattoos for my dad." He looked at me, then down at the paper. "Didn't get paid or anything, but it was cool seeing them on people."

"How does it feel to get one? Does it hurt?"

"Sit still. Yeah, it stings."

When he was through sketching, he showed me. "Like those pictures in comic books," I said. "It's great. Kind of a jazzed-up version of me."

Especially the chest. Wow.

"Yeah. I wouldn't mind doing comics or something like

that someday, but I can't think of how to write down the stories."

"Have you come up with any plots yet?"

"Sure, a lot of them. Like a series."

"I could help with that."

"Yeah?"

"Let's do it now. I'll get some notepaper, and you can tell me your story."

"It's about a guy stuck in this dungeon, put there by an evil spirit."

"Go on," I said.

"He only thinks he's locked up, but has the power to leave anytime he wants."

I liked having him with me. I felt relaxed. We didn't have to talk all the time. He poked around at the stereo system, looked at book covers. Sat on the back patio. Stared at the trees. Ate like a horse on its last bag of oats.

In my *E/Jones* journal I had a lot to write. Like a biography. Except with personal opinions. I knew nothing about his past. Evan didn't talk a lot, but I was starting to understand him pretty well. Zorro visited him almost every day at the cottage. Evan kept kitty treats in the kitchen drawer and asked in a high voice, "Does Zor Boy want a snack, huh?" Made me giggle.

In a way, Evan reminded me of my cat. Both came out of nowhere. Both depended on me, I liked to think.

I invited Bianca over as official math tutor.

She liked Evan. Really liked him. "He picked it up," she told me after the first time. "I don't think he's been in school much. That's the problem." After three sessions, Bianca said he pretty much had caught up with his class. But she came over anyway. I heard them laughing. Sometimes I stayed out of the way. After all, Evan needed more than one friend. Was I the slightest bit envious? Other times the three of us hung out, played cards. Evan sketched Bianca.

"If I really looked that good," she said, "I'd be happy the rest of my life."

Evan gave her a shy look. "You do."

During that time Tal came over most days after school. Just like before. We watched movies and music videos. Sang along. Laughed. Did English homework. "Man, these novels suck," he said. "I like true adventure stories. Who cares if the forest is a symbol? It's where bears live. That's all." Tal didn't know about Evan in the cottage. But Evan knew about Tal and stayed away when he was there.

I had a plan. Even ran it by Bianca. "Go for it!" she said with a wicked smile. I mean, here Tal was. With me every afternoon. For hours. Nice. Funny. But not a look. Not a touch. I was becoming seriously frustrated by our lack of progress.

One afternoon when we worked on study questions for "The Metamorphosis" and sat close together poring over our notes, I "accidentally" touched his forearm while reaching for a sheet of paper. Felt his warm skin under my fingers. Kept my hand there while looking into his eyes. To raise the ante, I had worn tight jeans and my most provocative top with the lace inset.

When a guy who makes a girl wobbly-kneed doesn't take initiative, it's depressing. Especially when the girl gives him all kinds of signals. Which I was trying to do now.

I didn't want a pal. I already had Bianca and Evan.

What happened then I couldn't believe.

Tal moved away from me and coughed.

Coughed!

As though I were infected.

I stood. Sucked in a huge breath. Said in a shaky voice, "Please stop coming here after school."

He looked like a little boy who had lost his pet frog. "What?" he croaked.

"Why do you come here?" I said, arms folded. "Let me guess. It's a good place to wait for the bus. You need help with dreaded English. You like the crackers and cheese."

"I told you, you're—"

"Comfortable." I let my arms drop. "So is a chair."

Tal pushed himself off the couch and backed up to the stereo. "I meant it as a compliment."

"Sorry. It doesn't work for me." My heart hammered. What was I saying? I felt like a bad driver trying to put on the brakes but hitting the accelerator instead. "You said I was your friend, but, truthfully, that's not how I feel about you. So it's not fair for me to be around you all the time when you don't—it hurts, that's all." I walked to the coffee table. Picked up my notebooks and a plate with leftovers on it.

He stared at me. "You want me to go?"

"Yes."

"Okay." His voice was quiet. He put his papers and books in his backpack and lifted it off the couch. Went to the door.

I was close to tears. "Is it my hair? My shape? My brain? Maybe you don't like girls with freckles. What's wrong with me?"

The look he gave me was actually . . . sweet. "Nothing," he said, "absolutely nothing," and closed the door behind him.

• • •

"He's an unfeeling robot," Bianca said when I called her. "Good riddance to Mr. Tal McTurkey."

Too bad I didn't agree.

That night Evan decided to shower and get to bed early. "I'm not going anywhere tonight," he told me. "It's so cool sleeping in a real bed and running real water on myself in the morning. It's like I want to take three showers a day and climb into bed just to feel the sheets against my back instead of a plastic bench."

I couldn't put it off any longer. I phoned Mim after he was gone. "Mom still isn't home. I'm calling the police."

Mim gave me a weird response. "Don't. Let me check a few things. Come over and sleep here tonight, Anne," she said. "I insist."

"This friend of mine, a guy from school, is staying in the guest cottage and keeping an eye out while Mom's gone."

"Do I know him?"

"No, but he's fine."

"He'll be fine if I say he's fine. Bring him over."

"Tomorrow, Mim. He's probably already in bed."

After hanging up, I called the Centerville Police Department anyway. Got a scratchy-voiced cop. Gave my name and address, my mother's name, and her last known whereabouts.

"She told you she'd be in Detroit and you weren't able to contact her?"

I said I had tried for over two weeks.

"I understand from what you've told me that she travels for business purposes. Has she always told you exactly where she'll be?"

"Not always."

"Could this be one of those times?"

"I don't think so. She's never missed my birthday before, never."

Silence on the other end.

"Sounds lame, I know, but my birthday was important to her."

"Are you alone?"

"My grandparents are nearby."

"That's good." Another pause. "We can't start a search for someone based on a missed birthday, especially when the person travels for a living."

"Can't you do anything?"

"I'll look into it. Give me a couple of days, and then we'll file an official report if she still hasn't returned."

Next afternoon, as I put my backpack down on the kitchen counter, my cell rang.

"Anne," Mim said. "I tried to locate your mom. Penny gave me an emergency number once. I'm sure it's probably a cell phone other than her regular one, but it might not be. I tried it. No answer. Actually, I got a recording that the number had been disconnected."

I took a deep breath to keep myself from shaking. "That makes two disconnections. We've got a problem," I said. "You know it and I know it. Mom always tells us when she'll be delayed."

"Anne, *please* come and stay with us until we find out. I don't want you over there all by yourself."

"I told you. I'm not alone."

"Ask your friend to keep an eye on the house. That way he could call if Penny comes back."

When Mim said "if," I had to sit down. "No," I said, "I'm staying here. I called the police last night, but they won't do anything about it for a couple of days. Mim, do you know a man named J.J.? He keeps calling here."

"J.J.? No, can't say I do. I'll ask your grandpa." She covered the receiver, and I heard muffled conversation. "No, he's never heard of him either."

"How about Diane?" I said.

Silence.

"Would my mother use it as an alternate name? A pen name?"

Nothing.

"How about Diane Stillman?"

I thought Mim would never speak. *Jeopardy!* blared in the background. "Diane Stillman is your mother's real name."

TWENTY-TWO

"WAIT! If Mom's real name is Diane Stillman, why isn't your name Stillman? Or was Mom married?"

"You'd better come over," she said. "We need to talk."

I left a note for Evan on the guest cottage door.

Evan,

I'll be home tomorrow. Spending the night with Mim and Gramps.

Anne

Both stood on the porch waiting for me. I followed them into the house. My stomach churned. I took off my sweater and put it over the arm of Gramps's rocker.

"Can I get you a Coke? Apple crisp? It just came out of the oven."

"No food. Talk to me," I said. "Tell me what you've never

told me before. Whatever you know about my mother. I'm about to go crazy."

The two perched on the fireplace hearth. The gold anniversary clock on the mantel chimed. Then its ticktock cut through the silence. Gramps pulled a handkerchief from his pocket. Pretended to blow his nose. "Mim, shall I?"

Mim gave him a stern look. "Make sure you say it right."

He sighed. "We figured someday you'd ask this question. Dreaded it, to be honest. You're a smart girl, and a lot of preparation went into guarding your safety. We were part of that."

"What do you mean?"

"Are you sure you won't have a drink of something before we get started?" Mim stood, dropped her needles and yarn into a basket on the table. "We could all stand a little boost."

I motioned for her to sit, which she did slowly.

Then I shouted, "No!" and jumped up.

"What?" Mim jerked to her feet.

"I don't know. I—I'm not ready. I can't hear it. Not now."

Gramps cleared his throat. "It's time, Champ. We promised her. Mim, we did promise Penny."

Something in the back of my throat had dried up. My voice came out in a squawk. "I only want to know if she's all right. Say she's all right. Please?"

"Let's sit and relax," Gramps said.

She'll call, I told myself. She wouldn't just forget me. "I've got to be alone right now," I said, grabbing my sweater. I put it on inside out.

My grandparents looked like old Raggedy Ann and Andy sitting motionless with their hands in their laps.

"I'm going back," I said. "Night."

Gramps shook his head. "You brought up the subject," he said. "Now it's out. We'll talk tomorrow."

"Yeah, tomorrow."

I had forgotten to leave a light on. The place was dark. Also the guest cottage. Zero messages on the answering machine. On automatic pilot, I went through my ritual of turning on the lights. My legs barely got me up the stairs. I crawled under the sheets.

I woke up to the sound of something breaking downstairs. At first I thought Zorro was roaming around, but then I remembered I had let him out. I sat up. Noticed 3:15 AM on the luminous dial of my bedside clock.

I stood rigid by my bed and listened. Had I dreamed the noise? A minute went by. Two. I heard footsteps coming up the stairs. The soft *pfft-pfft* of the plush carpeting mixed with the pressure on the wood underneath. I grabbed the bedpost and tried to think.

Mom! She had finally come home. I almost flew to the door.

I heard a whisper and a male's low voice. No, two!

My room is on the north side of the second floor. Three doors from my mother's. With back-to-back bathrooms in between. An open-to-the-first-floor sitting area bordered by the library across the hall. Ten feet from my door the staircase ends.

I had no choice but to try to bolt to her room before whoever was coming up the stairs reached the door. Naturally all the lights were on. I didn't touch them. I needed to hide. Knew where to go as long as I could make it.

As fast as I could, I slipped to the other side of my room,

against the wall toward the far doorway. Opening it, I stepped outside. Turned. Looked at the stairs. Saw two shadows rising toward the landing. I ran the rest of the way. Hoped I wouldn't fall. My nightgown wrapped itself around my legs. As I hurried into my mother's bedroom, I saw the two men enter mine.

My head ached. I felt nauseated and dizzy. Slipped through the closet door. Through the other door that led to the staircase in the back of the closet.

Who was upstairs and why were they here? How had they made it past the alarm system? What should I do now? Stay on the stairs or try to get out the back door and over to Mim's? Wake up Evan? Then a bolt of fear hit me. Evan! What if Evan was one of them? I really knew nothing about him. With the cell in my bedroom, the panic button under my mother's bed, and the other phone in the kitchen out in the open, I wondered how I'd call for help. I'd try the kitchen. Take the phone out the back door. Hope no one would hear me as I ran to my grandparents'.

I heard furniture moving. Objects hit the carpet. Sounds grew louder as the two entered the bathrooms, then my mother's room. They emptied drawers, threw them against the wall. I heard the clack-clack of microtapes as they fell on one another into a pile. "Lift that mattress up," one of them said. His voice sounded muffled. They entered the closet. I edged down the stairs. If they discovered the opening to the staircase, they would get me. The closet doors had no locks. Why didn't they have locks?

I pushed through the entrance to the semidark kitchen. The moon coming in the window sliced it in half. I stayed on the shadowy side as I crept to the phone and picked it up. Now, to escape out the back.

I crossed the room to the French doors, relieved that I made no sound. As I pulled the knob of the one on the right, I remembered the top latch was locked. I reached up with shaking fingers to undo it. The alarm system was disabled. *Click* echoed through the silence. I grabbed the knob, opened the door. Closed it as quietly as I could. Ran into the yard. My bare feet hit dry leaves and twigs on the cold ground. I looked toward the guest cottage. Bright lights—safety! Evan must have come back.

When I got there I could see clearly into the living room. Evan was not inside. I went around to the other window. Looked into the bedroom. Empty. I held the phone up to the light and dialed 911. One arm went around my waist. A hand over my mouth. I dropped the phone and heard "Nine-one-one. What is your emergency?" as I was dragged toward the big stone house.

TWENTY-THREE

"**COVER** her eyes." One of them, maybe both, had tied something over their mouths.

I could see nothing except the retreating lights of the guest cottage. Even that disappeared as something coarse went over my eyes and around my head. Ending in a knot in my mouth. I felt hands under my arms. Around my feet, lifting, carrying me back into the house. Up the stairs. The two put me on my bed facedown, where they tied me up after ripping up the top sheet. I managed to turn myself over on my back to breathe better.

"I don't know where else to look," one of them said.

"The bitch knows what she's doing. She's smart, but we'll get it."

"What if the cops come? We've been here too long."

"I'll decide how long. Go back in the other room and look again."

I didn't hear anything after that. Except for the thief in

my room. In the closet. Moving around hangers. Knocking down boxes off shelves where I kept newspaper clippings and photos. I heard the door of the small fridge opening and closing and felt a hand on my shoulder. Cold air hit my bare legs as he pulled up my nightgown.

"What else you got?" He undid the buttons on top. "Nice. Let's have a good look."

I could not move at all. I was cold all over and hardly able to breathe from the knot against my tongue. Gagging. I saw a faint dab of light from the lamp. By putting my head back I caught a single glimpse of a dirty blue-and-white-striped running shoe coming in the door.

"No!" the person entering said. "Don't do that. There's nothing else. It's probably not here. Come on."

"In a minute. I'm gonna have a little fun."

"No, don't."

I noticed it then. The faint sound of a siren. My phone number had been traced.

"We got to get out of here," the one by the door said. The other grunted and took his hands off me. I heard feet descend to the first floor, followed by silence.

I lay there without moving until the cold made me crunch up into a fetal position. Finally, I was able to get my hands in back over my feet and to the front. I undid the cloth over my eyes and mouth. Worked at the binding on my feet.

I looked around. Drawers out. Piles of papers. Laptop gone. Jewelry box dumped. Closet trashed. My mother's room. Worse. Her cassettes covered one part of the floor. Books scattered everywhere. I picked up *The Bookshelf*. Empty. I went back to my room and my little fridge and opened the freezer section. The Popsicle box was still full of the thousands transferred from the book.

Heavy feet of the law clomped through the front door and around the first floor. I grabbed my robe and went to the landing.

"I've been robbed," I said. Faces looked up at me and faded, melted into darkness. I fell.

Mim patted a cool washcloth on my face. "Anne, Anne. Why didn't you stay with us?" She sat on a dining room chair pulled up to the couch where I lay. A medic squatted next to me taking my blood pressure. I winced when he started an IV.

Mim's blurry face hung next to a policewoman asking me something. I couldn't hear. My ears roared. Glancing past her, I saw the hole where our stereo used to sit.

"If you feel up to it," Mim said through the fog, "the police would like to ask you some questions."

"All right." I tried to sit up. Big mistake. I felt as if a bowling ball had decided my head was a pin.

"You passed out," Mim said. "Bad bump. Good thing you didn't fall backwards down the stairs. The police said you slid on your side."

"How did you find out?"

"Your grandpa heard the siren and saw the police arrive."

I closed my eyes. "Mim, has Evan come in?" I tried to push myself up again, but the effort sent my stomach into a spin. She put her dry hand on mine and squeezed.

"You mean that boy staying in the guest cottage? How would I know if it was Evan? Someone did ask about you around ten minutes ago."

"Brown hair, really skinny?"

"Yes."

"What did he say?"

"Not much. He saw the police cars and wanted to know if you were all right."

"Where is he?"

A thin woman with a long, serious face, black eyes and hair, and bright red lipstick came over to me. "I'm Detective Emily Rodriguez." She slipped me a business card from the pocket of her navy jacket. "Who is Evan?"

"A high school boy living in the guest cottage out back," Mim said. "I'll get some fresh water for her head."

I looked around the living room. Destroyed. Bad enough to put Mom in a straitjacket. Drawers from the buffet table dumped all over the floor, pictures hanging crazy, papers and glass covering one chair, an overturned lamp. I groaned. Who could have done this?

"Before I contact him, I'll listen to your account," the policewoman said. Taking a pencil and pad of paper from her briefcase, she sat. Waited for me to begin.

In little bits, I told her.

"Do you notice much missing from the house?" Detective Rodriguez asked.

"Are you kidding?" I pointed to the room. "I keep this place neat. Upstairs it's even worse."

"Yes, I've seen it, but I don't know what's missing. You'll have to tell me, maybe when you've had more of a chance to look around."

"My computer for sure," I said, "and probably my mother's, and, oh, our outrageously expensive stereo setup. Some artwork."

"Did you recognize the suspect?"

"Two of them," I said. "No, they blindfolded me and disguised their voices by covering their mouths with something."

"Your house has a security system. It was turned off. Did you do it?"

"No. I heard someone out front last week late at night. Maybe that's when it happened, but we have a keypad, and I've never neutralized it."

The detective paused and wrote something lengthy. I watched her scribble. She was left-handed.

"Okay. Did either of the suspects try or succeed in assaulting you before or after they tied you up?"

I didn't like the queasy feeling the memory of that brought on. "One of them was going to. He had his hands all over me. The other guy told him to stop. They left when they heard the siren."

"Let's back up a little. You mentioned the suspects seemed to be looking for something. Is that what one said, that there was nothing else to steal?"

"Not exactly, just that they needed to go and that they hadn't found it."

"Do you have any idea what *it* is?"

"No." My head hurt so much I held my breath to keep from crying. I looked up at the white ceiling. It needed painting.

"Do you think they were men or teenagers?"

I thought for a moment. "I don't know."

"All right." Detective Rodriguez put away her notes. "We received a missing persons call from you concerning your mother. Sunday night, correct?" I nodded. "I saw it on our board this morning. I'm taking a personal interest in both areas, the robbery and your mother. I'll do what I can."

"Thank you," I whispered, trying to smile.

I liked this woman.

TWENTY-FOUR

YOU think you're that child, don't you? That Ruth begged me to raise her child because she had no one to give it to. Actually, she gave birth to a boy and died soon after of heart failure. Unfortunately, the baby had a defect that doomed him, too, several weeks later.

You came along as a result of my grief.

I saw myself as somehow responsible for Ruth's fate. The strain on her heart from the pregnancy killed her. I had practically talked her into her demise and was devastated. Ruth was my only friend, and I missed her terribly. The days blurred. I couldn't work or climb out of my depression.

Next door on my rather dismal street lived a family in a rental, with so many kids that I wasn't sure how many. I only knew too many. In those days I paid little attention to my neighbors, though those munchkins sounded like a fleet of fire trucks when they all decided to wail at once. After Ruth died, the mother of the brood brought me a peach pie and told me she felt bad for us, had learned from another neighbor that my roommate and her baby had died. "You miss them, don't you?" she asked. When I agreed the whole outcome was depressing, she whispered, "Bet you wish you had a little one to love."

I looked at her the way someone would regard a nutcase, said yes without a thought, and thanked her for the pie, which I ate in its entirety later that night.

Next month, the family moved out, taking everything they owned except one item in a corrugated-cardboard stewed tomatoes box.

A note was pinned to the blanket you were wrapped in. I never threw it away.

Miss Diane,

Heres Maryann. I know you will take good care of her. Dont try and find us. Thanx for your help. She behaves good.

You were screaming yourself purple at the time.

I could not remember the family's name or where they had gone. But why did I hesitate to notify the authorities? Maybe it was the thought that this dirty but darling child with fire shooting out of her head might grow up to write notes like the one above and I would be responsible for her lack of grammar skills if I gave her back. Or have several kids herself and never know what she could have become. I did make a few halfhearted inquiries, which did nothing to narrow the search. Your mother left no forwarding address, and she and her brood vanished. I had my suspicions that she might have been involved in welfare fraud. Regardless, I left my rental that day, taking you and what little cash I had. I could at least do something right in my life, something my parents had not ever considered in my case, and I started that day with you. Well, there it is.

Too bad it backfired.

Far away wasn't far enough.

TWENTY-FIVE

I sat in Mim's yellow-and-white-checked kitchen after breakfast the next morning. Sipped orange juice. It coagulated in my stomach. My head still hurt like crazy, and the roosters on the wallpaper didn't help at all.

Evan had disappeared. After searching the guest cottage, the police had found a small stash of marijuana, some clothes, nothing else. I had an appointment later that day with the police to list stolen items.

"You're never going inside that house again without Herman, the police, or me." Mim tossed her head. "You'll stay with us now. No arguments."

Both of them came to the table after the dishes and food were put away.

"How're you doing?" Gramps took my hand. "How's my little Champ?"

I couldn't help smiling. "You guys," I said, "I'm seventeen."

Mim pushed something imaginary around the plastic tablecloth. "We've been responsible for you for a long time. You're our Anne."

Gramps's voice cracked. "Been more a pleasure. By God, we have to keep you safe!"

"Herman, cut the melodrama."

"You're both the best," I said, taking my empty glass to the sink. "I'm ready now."

"Ready for what, dear?"

"For what you started to tell me last night."

Gramps shook his head. "We should wait until–"

"No. I want to know everything now."

"We don't know everything," Mim said.

Gramps rubbed one hand over his mouth and chin. "We'll fill you in on our part. That's all we can do."

"Your part?"

Gramps cleared his throat and nodded. "That's right, our part. Well, here's how it happened." He gave Mim a sad look. "Your mother came to me over sixteen years ago with a proposition. We lived on the same street in Milwaukee and chewed the fat often about this and that. I ran a little hot dog stand, and Mim here took in ironing. Penny bought lunch from me every day. I invited her to our place. The three of us got along, nice because we didn't have any relatives to speak of. Penny had a great sense of humor."

"Wait a minute. You two are her parents."

"Nope." Mim folded her arms. "You don't understand. We had been married–my first husband died–for about ten years. No children."

I sat and stared at both of them.

Gramps looked away. He always did when he didn't like the subject. "Penny's not our daughter. Our name's Johansen, not Stillman or Caldwell."

I couldn't say a word.

"We became good friends," he continued. "One day, she said she was looking for some nice folks to pose as her parents because her little girl needed an extended family. She also traveled a lot and wanted a stable place for the child to stay. We had been around you many times and thought you were cute and smart. We agreed to take care of you now and then. We didn't think she was serious."

Mim laced her hands over her knees. "She told us she had considered other couples, but I think she picked us because we had no other living relatives. We didn't realize saying yes to her meant moving so many times, but I know now that's what she had in mind."

I stood up. "Are you telling me you two and I aren't even *related*?" I walked out of the kitchen and into the living room, maybe to find a better answer there. I went back to the kitchen table.

Gramps motioned me to sit. "Blood doesn't always matter, Champ."

I remembered Mom's words: "You committed yourselves. Don't forget the perks." Now they made sense. "My mother made you promise not to tell, didn't she? So why are you doing it now?"

Mim nodded. "That was the arrangement, of course. But she said if something happened to her, we had to tell you."

"You think she's dead?"

Gramps rose, came over. Put a hand on my shoulder. "I'd

be surprised if that was the case," he said. "Your mother is street-smart. That's the best kind of smart."

I looked at the two of them. "What's going on with her?"

"Don't know." Mim rose, smoothed her pants. "She's never filled us in on her trips, and as you grew and we no longer took care of you as much, most of the time she stopped telling us where and when she was going and coming."

"Why did you tell me about yourselves, then?"

Gramps left the room. "Because," Mim said, "we promised. If your mother stayed away more than three weeks without calling, or if you became seriously worried and started asking questions, we were to tell and to give you a letter from her. We don't know what's in it, but she told us it 'explained things.' After you read it, you'll know the truth."

If she's a traveling writer, I thought, I'm a serial killer. Her last publication: 2000. Proof.

Gramps returned with a thick envelope. "Wait until you calm down before reading this," he said.

"Right," I mumbled, taking it.

I walked to my room to think. Turned around and went back to the kitchen. "How old was I when you first saw me?" I asked.

Gramps looked at Mim. "About seven months, right, Mim?"

She nodded. "You know, I never lived in anything over four rooms until we met your mother. We've had our moments, but throughout the years we've been fairly content. Penny is complicated. Yes, she is. We've always known that."

Mim put her arms around me, something she did not do

often. Her stiff hair brushed against my cheek. "It's about sifting. You have all the ingredients for life. Some are necessary for the mix, but others will ruin the taste. It's best to ignore those. Only put together the elements that won't make the cake go flat." She stepped back. Attempted a smile. "We four have had a good mix."

Mr. Harms would have liked that one.

I waited until late that day, after the inventory at the house. Told Mim and Gramps I needed to take a walk. Shoved the envelope in my jacket. Went past the downtown area into the park on the edge of town. Snow dusted the landscape. I pulled my jacket tight against my body as the wind picked up.

So here I stand on the hill. But the sharpness of the boulder does not hurt as much as the contents of the first half of the letter I have just read—twice.

My whole life is a lie. My mother's name: Diane Stillman. A woman with two lives and personalities. Mine: Maryann Somebody. A girl with a bunch of brothers and sisters. Two fictional characters. No, four! Mim and Gramps aren't my grandparents. And guess what? My birth date is probably wrong, too. How would Mom know it?

I clutch the letter. Halfway read. I can't finish it. Not until I get rid of the headache.

But that's not the reason.

I'm scared. If I read the rest, my life as I've known it will end.

A good life, really.

I don't know if I can face that.

Eleven-thirty. I start down the hill.

Now Evan is missing. My headache is worse. The letter inside my backpack: still half unread. What will I find scarier than the secrets already revealed?

Next morning, Gramps finds Zorro hiding under my bed in the stone house. He catches him with oven mitts and brings him and his litter box over. My cat is not happy. He sits with his back to me.

At night, Bianca and Mrs. Colon arrive with a pot of chicken tortilla soup, salad, cheese enchiladas, and sopaipillas. As we eat, Bianca questions me nonstop about the break-in. I let Mim answer. Bianca's mother shakes her head. "Is bad," she says.

Gramps serves himself a second helping. "Yolanda, this is excellent."

"Thanks, Mrs. Colon," I say. I try but can't eat.

"Is good? I make enough?"

"Enough for lunch tomorrow," Mim says.

Before they leave, Bianca corners me in the hallway, Grabs a handful of my shirtsleeve. "Are we best friends: yes or no?"

"That's a silly question."

"Do best friends rely on each other during rough times? Let me answer that. Yes. Have you been honest with me about whatever has been going on lately? No. You've shut down like the old west side roller rink. What's up, Annie?"

"Why are you holding on like a—an alligator?" I pull my arm away. "Stop it! If I had something to tell you, I would." I bite my lip to keep from crying.

"Sure," she says. She steps back as her mother comes in. Mim follows asking about recipes.

"Anne," Mrs. Colon says, hugging me, "you need something, you ask Bianca, okay? She tell me. I come. Remember."

I nod, look away. Bianca walks out behind her mom without another word or a glance back at me.

TWENTY-SIX

I have fallen asleep on the couch with my cell next to my face. The ringer makes my eyes fly open. I try to talk, but it comes out "Huhn?"

Tal's voice sounds far away. "I'm coming over."

"I'm not home."

"Yeah, I know. Bianca called me."

"She called *you*?"

"Be there soon."

"Wait—"

He hangs up.

Mim stands in the doorway. "Was that the boy from the guest cottage?"

"No. Tal," I say. "He wants to see me tonight and make sure I'm okay. Am I?"

Mim tilts her head. "You're fine. Where's that other boy? He seemed very upset when he asked about you."

"Evan? Really?" I sit up. My brain thumps inside my skull like a heart. "Wonder where he is."

Tal arrives fifteen minutes later. Gramps lets him in with a handshake and leaves the room.

I'm so glad to see him.

He looks way nervous.

"They tied me up and trashed the house. I got this bump from passing out after the police arrived."

Tal sits next to me. "Did either—uh—do anything to you? I've heard it's the MO of some burglars to . . ."

I feel my face go hot. "One tried, but the other stopped it."

He gets up and circles the living room like a caged animal. "Damn," he says, running his hand through his hair. "How did they get in?"

"Must have turned off the alarm system while I was here at Mim's."

He isn't looking at me at all, seems distracted. Swipes the air a few times with his fist and turns to me, his expression deadly serious. "Why were you in that house alone?"

I shake my head. "How did I know two guys were going to break in? Anyway, I'm the clumsy one for slamming my head on the staircase."

I've never seen Tal so angry, but I know it's not at me.

I see Mim through the kitchen doorway putting away dishes. "I don't care about that awful house. But I'm scared that . . ." The tears well up without warning. I cover my mouth, then wipe my eyes. "That my mother . . . Gramps says she's a survivor, but something's wrong. She's in trouble with evil people—I feel it—people who might have killed her." My words drop off to a whisper.

"What makes you think that?" He comes to me and pulls me up. "Come on outside for a few minutes where no one can hear us. Put on your coat."

Our breaths rise in streams of gray under the streetlight, my blood as cold as the night. "I'm freezing," I say.

He rubs my arms. "You'll get through this," he says. "Come on, let's go round the block." We walk to the corner. I stop.

"My headache's pretty bad. I forgot to take my meds tonight."

"We'll go slow. Come on."

"Why are you here?"

"Because I'm your friend."

I look up at the sky, see tiny pinpoints of light traveling with us as we start again. Past the Olson house with the red trim and stone walkway. Past Centerville Community Church where Mim and Gramps go sometimes. The Chamber of Commerce sign, then 7-Eleven.

"I called the police," I say. "Detective Rodriguez told me she'll help, but what can she do? Maybe Mom *is* stuck somewhere, or maybe an interview came up and she didn't have time to call."

He turns to me. "You don't believe that."

"No." I take a deep breath. "She's involved in something illegal. The only logical answer. If I'm right, I never could have predicted it, never. My mom is a little off the wall but so secretive. My own mother." I think of what I have just learned about her from the letter.

"Listen to me. You're not entering that house for any reason unless the police are outside or I go with you. Promise me."

I step away and look hard at him. "Why?"

"It's not safe."

"There's nothing left for anyone to take. I guess the robbers wanted something specific they didn't find, but I have no idea what it is."

"If you suspect your mother is into something illegal, maybe these men are involved somehow. Think. What could they want? Is there a safe in the house?"

"No, but . . ."

"What?"

"One time she left me a phone message telling me to look in the bookshelf. I practically took the whole living room apart, but what she meant was a book next to her bed with *bookshelf* in the title. I found thousands of dollars inside and a note that said I was beginning to understand. It's like a joke with her. I don't catch on fast at all."

"Did the money disappear in the robbery?"

"No, it was hidden."

"Where?"

"In the little fridge in my bedroom. I put it in an empty Popsicle box."

We have circled back to Mim's.

"Look," Tal says, frowning, "we could go over there now and pick up the money. It still has a chance of disappearing. Have your key?"

I nod. Tal and I start toward my house. Then I stop under a streetlight, and my hands drop to my sides. My headache is so evil I can barely see him. "What will I do without her?"

"You're strong," he says. "Your mother hasn't been around too much. But you've handled it."

I slide my arms around his waist. Bury my face in his chest. "I don't feel strong."

"Not now you don't. Your headache. The robbery. They'll go away. And your mom? Don't give up," he says. "Not yet."

I raise my eyes to his. Our faces are close, and my crazy brain wonders how he got such dark, curly eyelashes when mine are red and straight, and how I pinched my eyelid once curling them with that thingamajig Mom gave me. "What I said to you the other day?" I whisper, "I'm really sorry."

"No, Anne, *I'm* sorry." We pause while a car passes. Tal hugs me, and I feel his breath on the side of my face. I turn my head. His lips touch mine. So softly. My heart jumps a mile. I wait. For another.

But he steps away. "Let's get over there and make sure about that money," he says.

I'm disappointed. We walk on toward the house. Maybe when we're inside I will have the chance to tell him . . . and he . . .

I mean, what if he cares after all?

At the front door, I make a face. "Oh, no. I think I've forgotten the new code. Two-oh-three-eight? No, that's not right. Three-two-eight-oh?" I let go of Tal and pull the key from my pocket. He takes it and slides it in the lock.

"Wait! I have to enter the code. The alarm will go off."

I look up and see the door open, Tal's finger on the keypad. "What are you doing?" I ask. "How do you know—"

Click.

"Tal?"

"Let's go in," he says, giving me the key, his voice flat.

He stands there with his hand out. I heard it, the click when the code is right. How does Tal know it? Unless . . .

The key slides from my hand. I bend over to pick it up, but the sudden jab of pain in my temples makes it hard to see. The prickling sensation back of my nose, nausea like before the last blackout. I try to stand upright, but I'm sick, and my knees give way. I hear Tal say, "Anne, steady! Anne?" I sit down hard on the porch steps. Try to stay conscious. Listen to Tal's emergency call. He has a cell phone. Why don't I know that?

Then I see something in front of me on the porch. Two objects: Tal's dirty blue-and-white-striped sneakers.

I know.

"Here they are." Tal pulls me up as the ambulance turns into the driveway. "You'll be fine," he tells me. "I'll call your grandparents."

I'm on the way to the hospital. But not exactly sure where Tal has gone. After admitting me, the doctor in attendance calls my doctor. He orders me sedated for an overnight stay with a schedule of tests tomorrow.

In the morning the specialist tells me, "There's nothing to worry about."

I get a CAT scan. You have to lie perfectly still, headfirst in a tube. For at least twenty minutes. A million slices of your brain are photographed to a sound similar to a jackhammer. If you have claustrophobia, it gets better. During the procedure, every part of my skin decides to itch. Like a nest of fire ants having a smorgasbord. Later, back in my room, I try to sleep. Push away thoughts. Then I turn them loose to rattle around.

I make three calls.

"Gramps, will you go over to the house and get the Popsicle box out of the fridge in my bedroom? Then call me back, okay?"

Half an hour later, he says, "I found it, Champ. Why do you want an empty box?"

Next, I call Tal's home and get no answer. Third, I phone the police.

"I know who one of the robbers is," I tell Detective Rodriguez. "Talbot Haynes." I give the detective his address, settle back on my pillow. Cry until I can't anymore.

Tal deceived me from the beginning.

TWENTY-SEVEN

NO brain damage, the specialists decide. Nothing but a thwack on the head that will clear up with some rest. But my mother is missing. Evan, missing. Tal, who hasn't called or shown up, is missing with my money. Bianca. I'm missing her.

Back at Mim's, I realize my whole life has been full of missing people and places. All the moving, the friends dissolving into the landscape as we drove away. What and whom has my mother been running from? How could my grandparents pack up and leave all of those times without suspecting something?

Clerks in the attendance office at school know I won't be back until after Thanksgiving. My assignments come to me in fat, scary packets. The security company calls and tells me not even a wizard can break the code this time.

Evan has not returned to the cottage. What's happened to him?

Next morning, Gramps and Mim go out for Mim's annual checkup and Gramps's haircut. Three hours, they say, tops. Not much time for what I intend to do. First, I call Detective Rodriguez to find out what the police have done about Tal, but she isn't in yet. No one knows when to expect her at the office.

I take a quick shower. Throw on some jeans and a sweatshirt. Grab my car keys. Take off for Westfield. As I near the street where Tal lives, my throat goes dry. Tal's parents will hear just how much money their son stole from me.

Even before I pull up in front of the house, I know something isn't right. Leaves strewn around the yard by the wind press up against the front door. No car in the driveway. Windows with blinds pulled shut. I get out and walk to the door, knock and ring the doorbell. Go round to the back. One window has no blinds. When close enough to look into the family-room area, I see nothing. Literally. No furniture, rugs, people.

Pulling my cell from a pocket, I dial Rodriguez's desk. She answers.

"This is Anne Caldwell," I say. "I'm calling about Talbot Haynes. I mean, have you arrested him or talked to him about the robbery?"

Detective Rodriguez pauses. "We have no evidence besides yours that puts him at the scene," she says.

"Do you know he and his family have cleared out of Westfield? I'm here right now, and there's no one. The house is empty. I think it has been for days." I wait for a response but get none. "You don't know where he is, do you?"

Another pause. "Anne." She sounds careful. "This is police business. Leave the house. Go home and don't get yourself involved. We will handle the situation."

"What about Evan Jones?" I ask. "You don't believe he was involved in the robbery, do you, because I know he had absolutely nothing to do—"

"He's not a suspect at this time, but I advise you to tell him to vacate the guest quarters immediately. He has a record, and he's of legal age."

"A record? What did he do?"

"The State of Illinois sealed the file because the incident happened prior to his eighteenth birthday. I don't know how serious it is. But you should have nothing more to do with him."

"Have you learned anything yet about my mom?"

"Unfortunately, no, but you'll be the first to hear it if I do."

After Detective Rodriguez hangs up, I go to both of the neighbors' houses and knock. A middle-aged woman wearing a purple striped robe tells me she has been out of town the whole week and has no idea when the family left. The other woman, on her way out the door, gives me more specific information when I make up a story about searching for the boyfriend I haven't seen for quite some time.

"You poor thing," she says. "I'm afraid I don't have good news. I saw a police car there last week for—it must have been two hours. About a day later, the family just up and left without packing or anything."

"But there's nothing in the house. What happened to the furniture?"

The woman looks confused, then nods. "Oh yes, a storage company came and took everything a few days ago."

"What was the name of the company? Do you remember?"

She shakes her head. "Got a bad memory for names," she

says. "But what does it matter? I hate to say it, but I doubt you'll see them again, especially if your boyfriend didn't let you know where they were headed. I wish I could tell you more, but I never actually talked with them. They only lived next door for three months."

I thank her and walk toward my Jeep.

Three months.

What?

She calls to me. "For what it's worth, I think it was Fast Store or First Storage, something like that, dear."

I write the two names on a piece of scrap paper and start the engine.

TWENTY-EIGHT

EVAN is sitting at the kitchen table when I enter the cottage. His eyes have dark circles under them, and his hair is all messy.

I try to stay calm. "I thought maybe you'd at least check to see if I was all right."

He gives me a dark look and says nothing.

"Evan?" I sit next to him. He turns his head away. I don't need intuition to read his face. "Where have you been?" He shrugs, still doesn't look at me. "Where were you the night I was robbed?"

He puts his hands in his pockets and slumps. "Just down to 7-Eleven for smokes. When I got back and saw all the police cars, I got lost again—thought they were after me."

"I wish you'd have been home. *They* grabbed me here, right outside."

"Yeah, the cops told me. I'm sorry."

"But you could have come over to my grandparents' later. It's no secret where they live."

"I did."

"When?"

Evan shifts around. He puts both hands on the table then and looks straight into my eyes. "Twice. The first time your grandma said you were sleeping, and the second she told me to go away and never come back."

"Mim is overprotective. If I had introduced you to her, she wouldn't have said that."

Evan leans back in his chair and sighs like a rubber raft losing air. "Yeah, well, she's right. I'm no good. I came back here—I don't know—to think." He sets his mouth in a thin line and looks down. "I'm going in a minute."

My voice shakes. "I won't throw you out."

"I told that police lady I'd leave."

"You can stay. We don't have to tell anyone about it. As a matter of fact, I know who robbed me."

He looks surprised. "Who?"

"Tal—and someone else. He also stole some money my mom had hidden in the house."

"Man, that has to be hard."

I sigh. "It is. Anyway, stick around, okay? We're still friends, right?"

He nods. "Yeah, but I don't know. My dad's pushed me my whole life. My ma pushed me before she died. The school pushed me, and now—"

"I'm doing it, too."

He doesn't answer.

"You really feel that way?" A sob starts up in the back of my throat.

He shakes his head. "No."

I look down. "I heard you've been arrested before."

"Yeah. For possession. I also took a car for a joyride. Three months in Cook County Juvenile. Wasn't anything compared to what my dad did when I got out."

"I'm sorry."

He stands and stamps his foot. "Don't pity me! I'm letting you know how it is. Stay away from me. I'm going to try to stay away from you."

"Your past doesn't make any difference. You and I—"

"You and I *what*? Trust me. I'm no good."

"Evan." I turn my eyes away from his face. "I thought you needed me. But now, I mean, with my mom missing, it's good to have you here. If you go—"

"I know, but . . ." For a moment he looks helpless. Tries to smile. He sits down again and puts his head in his hands.

I fix my eyes on a branch outside the window. A blackbird looks in at us. Flies away.

I try to find the right words. Any words.

His chair scrapes the floor as he gets up and stretches. Before I know what I'm doing, I go and wrap my arms around him. Hug him tight. He is so thin. I feel his sadness in my bones.

He moves slightly. Puts his hands on my shoulders. Bends. Kisses my cheek first. Then my lips.

"Evan," I say, stumbling back, wiping my eyes, "no."

His face falls. He drops his arms, walks toward the door, pushes it open, runs out.

TWENTY-NINE

OH, it was hard caring for you. I had
no maternal instinct. You seemed to
know it and took advantage of my
shortcomings by crying the minute I
fell asleep, recovering just as I made
a doctor's appointment for a cough or
rash, staring at me with those big
green eyes the moment I resolved to
contact the authorities and admit I
had made a huge mistake. Immuniza-
tions? What kind? When? Equipment? I
bought a how-to baby book and managed
to make it through the first few months
of formula and rompers. But how would
I travel and write? It simply was not
practical to take you along, so I had
to find someone to care for you while I

was gone. You already know that story by now if you're reading this.

All went well. Mim and Herman entered our lives. Enough assignments came to me to keep us solvent even though we experienced a few rough periods where your chosen grandparents had to resort to their old jobs, which they willingly did to keep us all eating. We three worked it out. My own parents, drunks and freeloaders, had long since disappeared from my life, but these two loved you from the start.

Remember, Mim and Herman know absolutely nothing of what I'm about to tell you. They think I fly the world, interview, write, make incredible money by churning out insignificant biographies and hackneyed articles about has-beens. It's up to you to tell them the truth or to keep them in the dark. If I had worked exclusively as a ghostwriter all of these years, you would have eaten macaroni and cheese, worn JCPenney's your whole life, taken the bus to school, and thought you were lucky. What followed I did only when I had no other choice. No, my darling, though originally a writer, I found myself a new occupation, partly through the aforementioned suggestion

but primarily from a run-in with a
mother of many I hoped I'd never see
again.

I sit on my bed in the guest room reading Part Two of the
letter. Mim comes in with a visitor.

"Hi, Annie," Bianca says in a softer voice than usual. She
wears a wide-open expression like a fish for food at the top of
a tank. "What's up?"

I fold the letter in half. Shove it into my backpack on one
side of the bed. "Hi yourself."

"You two have a good talk," Mim says. "Would you like
to stay for lunch, Bianca?"

"I never turn down food. Lunch sounds great."

Mim tells us she'll call when the table is set.

"I never knew my grandparents," Bianca says when we are
alone. "Girl, you're lucky."

"You have no idea," I say. "Handpicked just for me."

Bianca plops on the bed and takes off her shoes. She lies
back on one of the lavender-flowered pillows. Puts her hands
in back of her head. "So, when's the big day they let you
come back to Lincoln?"

"After Thanksgiving."

"Way too long. How's your head? Did your fall knock
some sense into you?" She sits up suddenly. "I hope so, because know what? Tal's gone. Right after the robbery. It's
been a week. Have you heard from him?"

I pretend to laugh. "You mean the robbery where Tal ripped
my heart out of my chest and ran away with it?" I see his face,
feel his arms around me. Push both away. "Evan left, too."

"Yeah. What's with that?"

"I don't know."

"Annie, there's a reason I came over."

"It's great to see you! I feel so cooped up."

Bianca looks uncomfortable. She gets off the bed, lies back down and pulls a pillow over her head, then sits up again. "I need to tell you something. I'm jealous. I wonder why I can't get *my* heart broken like you. A guy like Tal would never look twice at me." She tilts her head. "You don't realize how pretty you are, Annie, and sometimes I feel left out of the looks department."

"Bianca, come on! Tal and I didn't get anywhere together."

She frowns. "Yeah, right. Anyway, the part about Tal kissing Shelley?" She grimaces. "I lied. Can you believe? They didn't kiss. They didn't even look interested in each other. That's it. You can disown me now."

Didn't look interested? Then why were they together? I never did quite believe the Westfield-connection story.

I shake my head. "It's over. He pretended to be all nice and concerned, but behind that face? He played me. You? You're too good for the guys at Lincoln. Romance will find you. Trust me."

"Oh, sure." Bianca steps away and sticks out her arms in an awkward pose.

"I mean it. You are going to be so beautiful in college that—that you'll be Miss January on the Urbana-Champaign coed calendar. The frat guys will beat down your door to date you, but we know you've got your eye on the young math professor with the Lamborghini, and he has both eyes on you!" Bianca lets out a loud laugh. I put an arm through hers. "Come on. Let's eat."

• • •

Bianca stays most of the afternoon. I need company, she says. Then gets to the gossip part of her visit.

"Mike Sherman about lost his Jockey shorts because he thought he was going to win the state history award," she says. "You haven't missed anything in English, though. We've been doing timed writing, and you know how we love that. Oh yeah, Junior asks about you every day."

I sigh.

"And every day I tell him to go jump."

While she talks, I sit back and decide. Mim cleans house on Mondays and won't let me help because I am still an "invalid." Mornings, Gramps walks downtown with happy bottles clinking in his pockets. Spiked coffee with the seniors at Hank's. Tomorrow I'll make my move. My grandparents won't know where I've gone.

Next day, I strip the bed, dust-mop the floors of the guest room. Afterward, I call to Mim that I'll be back in an hour after a walk. Wearing a heavy ski jacket, I step into the cold November morning. My breath comes in short, white puffs. A dusting of snow that looks more like frost covers the neighborhood. Fog hangs down so thick it makes the houses I pass look as if they're hidden behind thick gray veils.

The letter that I want to finish but can't seem to sits deep in the backpack, now slung over one shoulder. My assignments are on the desk back at the house—fifty pages in history. Half of *Things Fall Apart* (no kidding). Math problems. French translations. New passages of music. I think of Beastie Boy freezing in the back of my Jeep. Being away from school is easier than I thought, though. In fact, I feel somewhat liberated.

• • •

I check the cottage first, glance in the rooms. Evan's books, clothes, cigarettes are gone. The place is cold, empty, except for one thing: the drawings and story we worked on.

Around front, a policeman sits in an unmarked car as usual. I say hi and wave. He nods. I unlock the door of the main house, punch in the code. Something jogs my memory as I enter the place, that feeling the first time Evan went in with me. I know now what it was: the familiar click that the correct code causes. Because the system had already been disabled, I hadn't heard it, even though the red light had changed to green. Tal and his fellow thief must have had expert knowledge of a system like ours. Tried it out before the robbery. Afterward, he was able to bypass it again.

The stone house is cold. Someone, probably Gramps, has shut off the heat. The living room with little light coming through the windows looks dismal. Nothing has changed. Books, papers, shattered glass everywhere. Like someone threw Mom's stuff around to have fun breaking it.

The electricity has not been disconnected. I see the blinking red light on the phone. I remember that my cell needs charging. Haven't turned it on for a week. Not sure why.

Two messages. Maybe one from Bianca. Probably before I moved in with Gramps and Mim.

I push the button.

"Anne."

I catch my breath. "Anne." Tal's voice, soft. "I know you'll hear this. You'll come here alone. Be careful. Stay away." Strange thing for a crook to say. After about ten seconds, he adds, "And don't think for the rest of your life that I'm—uh—all bad."

"Wednesday, 9:45 AM," says the generic male messaging-system voice.

The day after we saw each other for the last time.

Before I can stop the machine, the next message begins. The hairs on the back of my neck prickle.

"Diane's daughter, right? Listen carefully. She owes us. We *own* her. You know where she is, and you *will* tell her J.J.'s coming."

Time: last night at 8:17. His accent isn't from around here. I hope he lives far away.

The house is so quiet that I hear myself breathe. I look around. Take the stairs two at a time. Go straight to my mother's bedroom, where I see, in piles on the floor just as they were after the robbery, the microtapes Mom used to do her interviews. I scoop them all up, drop them into my backpack. Those in her desk also go into the pack. Nowhere in any of the drawers do I find a player. I'll have to get one later. Maybe I won't find anything on the tapes. But it's a place to start.

Before I leave, I dial Information. "I'm looking for a Fast Store or First Storage," I say.

"City?"

"I don't know—maybe Westfield."

"One moment. I have a First Storage in Centerville. The number is—"

I punch it in and wait.

"First Storage. How can I help?"

"Our things were picked up a few days ago, and I forgot how long it would take for them to reach us."

"Your name?"

"Haynes."

"Just a second." I'm on hold for a few minutes. "Ma'am?

We have no customer on record by the name of Haynes. Do you have the right place? Our company *rents* furniture for short periods. We do not transport it anywhere but back to our building."

"I must have the wrong company," I say. "Thanks."

I remember the cheap paintings, the lack of reading material, the motel look of the house. No wonder. Was the whole family in on it? What was their purpose in Westfield? To clean us out?

I call Westfield High, make my voice as adult sounding as I can. "This is the records secretary from Lincoln in Centerville. We still have not received Talbot Haynes's transcripts, and he has been with us since September. Will you check that for me?"

I feel a twinge when the woman on the other end asks me to wait.

She comes back on. "We've never had a student named Talbot Haynes. Are you sure you have the correct high school?"

I lock up and go back to Mim's, hear echoes of Tal's voice saying "Anne" twice. "Don't think for the rest of your life that I'm—uh—all bad." That statement can only mean that I will never see him again.

Should I call Detective Rodriguez about J.J.? Is he on his way, and if so, does he know where my grandparents live? Will the police be able to protect us? My head pounds. What should I do?

I near Mim and Gramps's house. See a squad car parked out front. Detective Rodriguez comes out the door, her expression grim as she walks to meet me. Gramps is behind her. Followed by Mim.

I know.

THIRTY

AT the walkway to the house I stop.

I'm not ready for it. It can't be true. Detective Rodriguez wears an I-hate-to-have-to-say-it frown. Official. Final.

I start to shake. "You're here about my mom."

"Inside, Champ," Gramps says. "It's cold."

"Wait. What happened, Detective?"

She nods. "I'm sorry to have to tell you that officers found your mother this morning outside Kansas City in a wooded area."

The backpack slides off my shoulder onto the sidewalk.

"Let's go inside."

"How did it happen?"

"Anne," Gramps says.

"Tell me."

"One shot to the back of the head. It appears to be a contract killing."

"How do you know it's her?"

"She had ID on her as well as some documents bearing her name."

I look at my grandparents, remember they have no idea my mother's life took a turn. One that should become clear when I finish her letter. Never mind the fights. They're as loyal as retrievers.

"What will they do with her? I mean, will she be sent here for—"

"Yes, as soon as the autopsy is complete, we'll let you know, and her remains will be shipped back. At that time you'll need to identify the body, a formality, of course. Did your mother tell you her burial preference? Did she leave a will?"

I can't get my head together. My mind is as blank as a white sky in winter. Then I recall the night at Mama Leone's, the will, the bank statements. Could she have predicted her death at that time? It seems either creepy or *way* coincidental.

"Yes, both," I say.

"Come on, let's go inside now," Detective Rodriguez says, "and warm up." She walks to me, picks up my backpack. I feel her hand on my shoulder. The first sob broadsides me, and I lurch forward as it leaves my body in a wail. I don't even recognize my own voice.

Her hand goes around my waist to steady me. "I can recommend a grief counselor." Her voice is cool but reassuring. "This is a big burden for a girl so young."

"I don't want counseling." I wipe my eyes. "Detective," I whisper so that my grandparents can't hear, "this guy J.J. left a phone message at the house threatening me. He says my mother owes him something and that I have to tell him where she is."

"You didn't erase it, did you?"

I shake my head no.

"Okay then. I'll go over and listen to it. Don't worry. We'll find the guy."

I walk inside after Mim and Gramps. The detective follows us. She stands while the three of us sit on the couch.

"I'll do everything I can," she says, "but since your mother was murdered out of state, this is a matter for the FBI. Whatever they tell me I'll pass on, but sometimes we don't get any information from them until they're good and ready."

"We understand," Gramps says.

After the detective leaves, the three of us stay in the same spot. Hunched together. I cry, then stop. The room is dark and quiet as an empty church except for the ticking of the anniversary clock. Gramps's mouth is a thin line. Mim's head is bowed.

"Penny gone," Gramps says later at the table. "I can't believe it."

"Shush, Herman!" Mim snaps.

I reach across the table and take her hand. She looks deathly white. "Mom left money," I say. "I've seen her will and bank accounts. Don't worry."

"But with what you know about us—"

"You two are heroes in my book. According to Mom's letter, her birth parents were awful."

"She never mentioned them," Mim says. "Have you finished it, the letter?"

I force a smile. "It's like lima beans, something you can only stomach a little at a time."

"I've always liked lima beans," Gramps says.

"What don't you like?"

"Eggplant."

155

"You never told me that, Herman!"

"Eggplant, then," I say. "The letter is like eating eggplant."

Later, while getting ready for bed, I ask myself, Why read the rest of the letter? Then I wonder why I can't finish it. Same reason I push away memories. I'm afraid. What do I think I'll find? And what about the tapes? Are they important?

Penny Caldwell is gone. I see her face. Blank without the smiles. Eyes that never missed anything, now staring at nothing.

Mom is dead.

Most of the night I cry into my pillow so Mim and Gramps won't hear me and get upset. I need to sleep. Zorro jumps up on the bed, nestles near my neck. His purrs help me drift away. Push sadness into blackness.

"Your mother was always home for Thanksgiving," Mim says the next morning at breakfast. "Never missed a one. Shall we still have dinner? She would want us to."

"I don't know." My eyes are puffy. "Maybe we should skip this one."

"And sit around feeling sorry for ourselves?"

She has a point. "If I knew where Evan was, we could invite him, too."

Mim wipes her mouth and smashes her napkin in a ball. "I met him. He tried twice to see you, but I wouldn't let him."

"He told me." I get up, clear the table. Cry. Try to keep it quiet. My voice is shaky. "I'll go turkey shopping with you today. Do you want me to?"

"Nope. Get some rest."

I sob. Mim comes to me, holds my face and wipes my tears with her fingers. "We'll get through it," she says.

THIRTY-ONE

WE were more or less established and happy in the Milwaukee area, we four completely nonbiological "family members," when a man I'll call Luke contacted me. He said he was a friend of a friend of a friend and hinted that I had shown an interest in an excellent though risky "travel" proposition mentioned a year or two back.

"What are you talking about?" I asked, and when he connected the dots for me, I said, "I remember, but I've got a kid now. I can't do something like that. She might find out someday and hate me."

My precious, do you see the irony?

Give me credit. I refused the temptation initially. But then your birth mother tracked me down. I think she might have tried the same scam with some of her other children as well, because the lady was all business. She put it this way: "Give me ten thousand dollars or I'll take her, and there's nothing you can do about it."

In those early days I had five hundred dollars in a savings account that I filched from every other month. Mim took in ironing and Herman had a part-time job as painter and groundskeeper at our apartment complex. You had two outfits that we washed every other night. Even though I assured the lady I had no money, she clung to me like a tick. I could not get anywhere with this woman, who held the threat over my head like a wrecking ball ready to drop. Finally, panicked at the thought of losing my flame-haired darling, I told her I would see what I could do about raising some cash, a ploy to stall her.

One morning I dug out the card the friend of a friend of a friend had shoved into my hand, the scrap of paper I almost had thrown away, and dialed the number. When Mr. Anonymous explained the turf to me, the job didn't seem so bad. I would even have a title: courier.

Soon I was flying off. My travels took me overseas to fabulous resorts in Mexico, to Canada, to Indonesia, to the French Riviera. Of course, my writing career died a sad little death, but the way the money rolled in, who cared? I told myself I could go back to it someday, write the great American novel and all that.

I moved us back to Illinois after a time, but she found me again, saw we were living better, and demanded more. I swear she had hired a private detective, because she showed up at the same time of year like a debt collector. But now she wanted twenty thousand dollars. You're probably thinking, Why didn't Penny sic a couple of goons on this woman, threaten to do away with her if she came anywhere near us again? The answer is simple. I didn't want anyone to know where you came from, not the boss, not even Mim and Herman. The less anyone knew about me, the less I would be accountable for, and the safer you would be.

However, when your birth mother turned up for the third time twelve months later, her scrawny hand reaching out for fifty thousand dollars, I told the friend of a friend of a friend to get her out of my face without hurting her. I concocted a fairy tale about a deranged stalker who thought you were her baby(!) and planned to abduct you. Mission accomplished.

Two more years went by. You grew into an adorable child who loved school and the whole world around her. We four had a good life. My employers considered me an expert, increasing my take depending on the cargo: drugs, jewels, documents. (I was only the messenger, not the consumer, after all.) During those years I put away a bundle of money but always kept cash in a variety of locations in case I had to grab you and run. Wherever we went, I kept my eyes on rearview mirrors and corners of buildings.

And then, disaster.

One day when I least expected it, he showed up. We had stopped at a gas station. You stayed in the car while I went in to pay and get you some ice cream.

This man, shaggy-haired, muscular, with tattoos everywhere but his face, is the sort of lowlife I used to see outside my first apartment in Chicago.

He walks toward me, points at me with a long, dirty nail, and stands so close I see yellow in the whites of his eyes. Next to him a boy of about ten wearing a Ninja Turtles sweatshirt, his son I presume, takes a bag of M&Ms off a shelf, rips it open, and pours the candy into his mouth. When I look at him, his eyes dare me to say something. He knows the ropes, I tell myself.

"You think you can hide," the man says, "but I found you anyways, Diane Stillman. My wife died because of you. That's right. Had a heart attack when you sent them men to threaten her."

I had no idea the woman had a husband.

The boy stares at me. I slip by the pair and step to the counter.

"You have my girl," the man says when I turn toward the door, "and I want a hundred thousand dollars or I send the law after you. I know you got it."

Naturally, I deny everything, my name, you, any money I might have, but this man is as mad as a hornet and beelines outside after me, followed by the kid, who—get this—pulls a pack of cigarettes from his jeans pocket and lights one up.

This ten-year-old has a tattoo on his right forearm, and I'm about to ask his dad if it isn't a little much along with the ciggie hanging out of his mouth. But I keep my opinions to myself, except to say, "I have no idea what you're talking about. I'm going to leave now."

I hurry to the car and drive away, but I know it's him, and I know we have to leave as soon as possible. Thank my common sense, I think, as I break the speed limit on the way home to pack, that I formally changed my name from Diane Stillman to Penny Caldwell. He won't find me again, I promise myself.

But he did find me. Seven years later this maniac showed up, last fall to be precise. I had to do everything I could to stop you from learning the truth.

I put down the letter. Hear myself breathing. Hard. No. No! That's not all that happened. There's more, much more.

It all comes back to me in a terrible rush, the day at the gas station when Mom told me about the rude man who wanted her gas pump. She got in the car, handed me the ice cream bar. We smiled. Suddenly his face was at her window. Ugly. Skin pulled back. Cheekbones like chiseled rocks. Square teeth. Mouth twisted with hate. He reached in and grabbed my mother by the throat.

"You'll be sorry, bitch," he whispered.

I screamed. His eyes like black stones locked on mine. He grinned, and I saw it coming out of his gray shirt. The snake head. "Well, look at you, little princess," he said, squeezing harder.

My mother was choking, trying to pry his hands away. He held on. I screamed again. And again. Looked out the other window for help. The lot was empty like the surface of the moon. Except for the boy. He stood next to a gas pump staring at us. Helpless. That's what he was. Frozen in time. He put up his hands, face pale, scared. Like he wanted to say something. Do something. But couldn't.

I looked at her purse beside me. Dropped the ice cream bar on my shorts. Reached in the side pocket, my hand shaking so much I could hardly grab the key ring. But I pulled it out. Shoved the key in the ignition. Turned it. The car started.

My mother managed to put it in reverse with one hand while pulling at the man's hands with the other. He stumbled as she made the car jerk back and forth, and finally he let go. She peeled out of the gas station. I turned around and saw him, fists in the air. Yelling. His face in a terrible rage. The boy, still in the same position like a statue.

Mom raced back to our house. Coughing and gagging. We packed up and left that night, Mom still rubbing her neck as we flew down the highway.

Over and over, I pointed to headlights behind us. Screamed, "He's coming, Mommy, he's coming to get us!" Gramps pulled me into his lap. Buried my head in his chest. Sang, "Do your ears hang low? Do they wobble to and fro? Can you tie them in a knot? Can you tie them in a bow?" until I fell asleep.

The next morning Mom told me we were far away now, that she would protect me from the bad man.

I shrugged. Wondered what she was talking about.

THIRTY-TWO

THE house is quiet with Mim out shopping and Gramps down the street with his buddies. I think about what I have just read. What I know.

Penny Caldwell was a courier who transported illegal stuff either from the United States to other countries or between American cities. I didn't have to hear much of J.J.'s voice on the answering machine to know just how deep my mother had sunk into the mud.

I slip out, drive to Wal-Mart, where I buy a cheap tape player with earphones and a large pack of AA batteries. Back at the house, I close the door in my room and put in the first tape. Ellen Andrews. I hear two female voices, one Mom's. Chef Ellen grew up in Philadelphia, worked in her dad's hoagie shop until she had a chance to go to culinary school in the seventies.

The food talk makes me hungry. I smear a bagel with chunky peanut butter, resume listening. If the tapes last thirty minutes on each side, it will take me until Christmas to listen to them. Sometime during the second tape, I fall asleep.

I say no to lunch. Plug myself into homework. Somehow it doesn't seem relevant to my real life. I wade through it anyway—math problems, a chapter on Reconstruction after the Civil War. I read the same two paragraphs three times, close the textbook. I take out the list started in the library that day during lunch. In the minus column my questions have been answered. I decide to add to it.

Mom

+	–
• *employed in steady career:* ~~lots of books to show for it~~ *date of last book published: 1995. Nothing after 2000.*	• *writers don't stash thousands in hollowed-out books*
• ~~interviews out of town~~ *but says it's necessary*	• *does not inform me of whereabouts*
• ~~good mother~~	• *never talks about her past*
• *tried to protect me*	• *no wonder: broke the law*
• *set up financial security*	• *it's money she got illegally*
• *made sure I had "grandparents" to care for me*	• *she should have told them the truth and given them a choice*

I slip the paper in the notebook. Put my theories on hold. After this weekend, back to school. Back to my life. Without Mom. Without Tal. Without Evan. Without a real family. I want to tell Bianca everything.

What if I do? I can see it: she and her mom asking me to move in with them. The Colon method of handling issues—yell, cry, kiss, feed, yak. I love that family, but I—not to mention my jumpy cat—couldn't live in a house where noise equals breathing. Or could I? At the Colon home nobody is lonely. You can bury bad memories in the commotion. In the hugs. In the tortillas.

Did my mother know she was in enough trouble to share her financial situation with me that night at the restaurant? It seems so. Money. That's one thing I won't have to worry about. The thought doesn't make me feel any better.

Monday I'll call the lawyer, I think. Ask him to sort out everything for me according to Mom's will. If Gramps and Mim don't own their home outright, I'll make sure that they do.

As for me, what's next? Sell the stone house? Wait for Detective Rodriguez to find J.J.? If not, give him money to leave me alone when he shows up? I'm sure I can live on my own until graduation. I practically have anyway for the last two years.

But those in-between times Mom stayed around, it was good. More as friends than as mother and daughter. She trusted me to make the smallest of decisions. Yeah. My future will be full of decisions. She trained me well that way.

Evan. Money won't solve his problems. He needs someone to care about him. Where is he? What if he comes back? I could get him a tutor. I could try to teach him myself. How do I feel about Evan anyway? I don't know. I'm so mixed up. Could it be that way? He does mean something to me. But what? I think of the kiss. Hmm. There is a connection. But a connection I can't even explain to myself. I knew it the first time I caught him staring at me.

For now, I have the funeral and the key to the safety-deposit box: Mom said directions for her cremation and burial are in it. After I identify the body, I'll take care of that.

• • •

Next morning I awake to the smell of turkey. I pad into the kitchen. Mim already has her best china and silverware piled on the table. Leaves, berries, and candles decorate the middle of the white linen tablecloth. Mom did not cook much, but she loved formal dinners. Mim and Gramps always in their best clothes, Gramps's finger yanking at his shirt collar. I even got to sip a little wine on these occasions. Mim hated that. Mom thought it was cute.

"Four o'clock can't come soon enough for me," Gramps says from the living room. "Smells like heaven, Mim."

She walks in from the kitchen. "I always wondered what heaven smelled like. Now it doesn't do me any good." She looks at me. "You'll feel better if you dress up today, Anne."

"I will. Can I help with anything?"

"Would you like to learn to make Waldorf salad? It's easy. Apples, nuts, celery."

I nod. "I'd better learn to do a lot of things now, huh, Grandma Mim?"

She gives me a wry look. "I like hearing that."

"What, that it's time to grow up and make my way down the dusty road of life?"

"No. I like the fact that I'm still your grandma."

Later when I enter the dining room dressed in a skirt and lacy shirt, Mim is smiling.

The table is set for seven. I look around. "What's going on?"

The Colon family comes in from the living room. "Surprise!" they yell. Miguel hops. Bianca grins. Mr. Colon, in a suit, walks very straight, his hair slicked back like an old-time movie star's.

"Mim and Herman invite us," Yolanda Colon says. She

holds out her arms. Hugs me. "We all have lotta fun, no? And cheer up our Anne."

"I propose a toast to Penny Caldwell," I say later. At holiday dinners, we always toast something or someone. I hold up my wine glass with the swallow poured in the bottom. Except I'm seriously fuzzy. I emptied a few of Gramps's little bottles while I dressed. "To Penny—who tried," I say.

"Who tried what, dear?" Mim asks.

"Who tried to hold it together."

"That's right!" Gramps shouts. He's had his share, too.

"To Penny. *Salud!*" the Colons say in unison.

Everyone yaks and laughs. I work my shoes off under the table. Rub my feet together like a cricket to some corny background music Gramps put on. For a while, I forget. After dinner, Mr. Colon serenades us with Mexican folk songs. His voice is deep and mournful. Miguel plays chess with Gramps. Mim and Yolanda Colon clear the table and wash the dishes. "You and Bianca. You go talk girl talk," her mother says.

Out on the cold porch, Bianca pulls out a quart of tequila and some cut-up limes with sugar on them in a plastic bag.

"Cool," I say, still dizzy from Booze Buzz, Part One. After a couple of shots I start to blubber. "Mim calls people like me crying drunks. She hates them."

"Aw, come on, Annie."

"You guys are a real family. Why can't I have one like yours? I feel so—empty."

"Hey, wait, lady." Bianca caps the bottle. Puts it down beside her. Pats my tears with her sweater sleeve. "For one thing, nobody's family is perfect. Take mine. Mama monitors me like a newborn—you know that. And my papa? Well, let's just say he's got more rules than the pope."

She hugs me and I hold on. It calms me down a little. "Those grandparents in there are as good as it gets. I know your mom's gone, but she didn't have as much to do with you as they did. Tell me I'm wrong."

I put my face in my hands and sob.

"Oh, I know. You think if she had loved you, she would have stayed home. You could have had more of a relationship, right? But guess what? If she had been around all the time, you would have been the one taking off. That's how it works."

My brain is clogged like a sink full of hair. From somewhere I think, She's right.

"Anyway, your mom loved you. A lot. I saw it. Bottom line: Someone had to bring home the bucks."

"Oh yeah. Lots 'n' lots of bucks," I say. I get up, squint. The streetlight looks like an enormous metal garbage-can lid, all lit up. I run and throw up in the bushes next to the house.

"Take two aspirin, a spoonful of sugar, and a vitamin before bed," Bianca says under her breath as she and her family leave. "You'll feel great tomorrow."

I did. And I do.

How does she know this stuff?

It's morning. I leave the house early, plan to head down to Midland Park and back. My feet turn right, almost by themselves, at the end of the street. I'm in front of the stone house waving at the unmarked car, then inside the front door staring at the same mess.

I tiptoe to the phone. No new messages. Good: I won't have to listen to Tal's voice again. Good: J.J. has given up on me. Or, good: Detective Rodriguez has nabbed him and forgot to tell me. Bad: J.J.'s on his way. The thought sends a chill through me. But it doesn't stop my feet from running up the stairs to my mother's room.

What am I searching for? Anything. Anything that will help me understand what Penny Caldwell did all those years. But how can I find information like that, especially after a robbery? What were they looking for that night? What was the "it" they referred to? Tal could tell me, but I won't see him again. I have to face that fact. No matter how it hurts. And it does. So much.

Around the bedroom, my eyes stop on things dumped out of drawers, strewn on the floor, on the desk and dresser. Clothes, papers, CDs, books, perfumes, cosmetics, pencils. I go to the huge closet. Clothes spill out of built-in drawers or lie in wrinkled heaps on the floor. One by one I sift through the piles, empty the contents of each drawer, put them back.

Now the closet is neat the way my mother liked it. I see her favorite sweater, mint green with yellow flowers and gold sequins. I put it against my face. Hug it. Breathe in the faint smell of her skin. My eyes fill. I fold the sweater carefully and put it away. Toward the back I find three boxes of newspaper clippings, photos, office supplies. I drag each one into the bedroom. Make a fast search through.

This is crazy, I think. What am I looking for?

Next, I go through her desk and dresser. The only important item I find, a single microtape in the back of a desk drawer, goes into my backpack.

THIRTY-THREE

THE rest of the weekend, I catch up on homework. To Zorro's disgust, I even practice Beastie Boy. Each night I listen to tapes. Penny had interviewed a ton of people. Some tapes are halfway interesting. But I don't find information that will help me understand what happened to her.

Sometimes I drift. Wonder where Tal and his family have gone. Remind myself again it's over. Still, I think of the day he walked into the band room. The way he paused, put down his trumpet case. He scanned the room, turned his head from one side to the other, stopped when he saw me as if he were looking for me. It only lasted a moment. Strange that I remember it now.

The letter. I definitely have a psychological block. The sight of it makes me nauseous. But what more can it dump on me? I already know my grandparents were manufactured. Penny Caldwell had kept a baby (me) belonging to a greedy birth mother who blackmailed her. Penny herself turned criminal to pay her off, then sent guys to threaten her. It caused her death, said the woman's husband.

Where has he gone? Did he find us after we moved to Centerville? Did Penny send more troops to get rid of him as well? Or did she pay him off?

Monday, Mim tells me the three of us are to report to the morgue as soon as possible to identify the body.

"Also," Mim says, "Penny's lawyer would like to see you tomorrow morning. I told him he'd have to make it after school because you'd missed too much recently. Did I say the right thing?"

"You always say the right thing." I look at the paper. Four o'clock. I shove it in my pocket.

"How was the first day back? Did everything go all right?"

First time in school in over two weeks. I felt like a stranger. Mr. Washington met me coming in the door. How did he ever find big enough clothes? He didn't seem to know what to say to me. I felt a little bad for him but started to walk away.

"Just a minute, Anne." He hurried to catch up. "You've had it rough with the robbery." He stood on his toes and rocked back on his heels, searching for words. I was afraid he would fall backward like a top-heavy, roly-poly toy. "Your mother. Let me offer my deepest condolences."

I nodded. "Thank you. Does everyone at Lincoln know?"

"It's been on the news. Truthfully, I'm surprised you're here."

"Do you know Evan Jones?" I asked. "He's a friend. I was wondering if you've seen him."

Mr. Washington frowned. "Jones? He hasn't been in school for two weeks. If you find out where he is, let me know. We've been trying to locate him ourselves."

Throughout the day, I saw sympathetic looks. At one point, I ducked into the restroom and cried in a stall. Mostly for Mom. Or from fear. Bianca kept her usual vigil over me the rest of the day. Junior came up at one point and said, "Hey, Anne, I heard. Sorry, man."

"Just a normal day at school," I tell Mim and Gramps en route to the morgue.

When we arrive and enter the building, I turn to my grandparents. "Would you mind if I went in alone?"

Gramps says, "Go ahead. We'll wait right here."

"I'm here to identify Penny Caldwell," I tell the officer at the front desk. "I'm her daughter, Anne Caldwell."

Nodding, he motions for me to follow him down a hall. We push through a double door. The officer goes to a desk by a large window. Talks into a microphone. "Penny Caldwell," he reads off a paper on a clipboard. He turns to me. "Ready?"

Approaching the window, I see the gurney. Like one on TV with the draped body waiting for identification. A woman wearing a lab coat stands next to the cart, her hand on the sheet. She raises her eyes, kind of sympathetic, to me as she reaches to lift the cover from Penny Caldwell's face.

"Wait. I just need to—"

The officer puts up one hand to signal the woman. I turn. Try to keep my legs from giving way. "Take your time," he says.

I lower my head. Feel my face drain. I'm cold all over. I don't know how long I stand there taking deep breaths.

"All right," I say finally.

Suddenly, another police officer comes in. "I'll take it from here," he says. "Just a minute." He gestures to the woman to pause. Then he switches off the microphone. "Turn so your back faces the window." When I do, he says, "You will find something other than you expect. Just bear with us, Anne. Do you think you can? Please keep what you are about to see to yourself."

"What do you mean? Is she all messed up? Won't I be able to recognize her?"

"That's not it. Just turn around, look, and nod. Can you do it?"

"I guess, but—"

The officer waves to the woman in the lab coat. She lifts the sheet and folds it back to provide me a full view of the face.

I swallow. Hard.

"Come on," I tell Gramps and Mim as I hurry through the door into the waiting room, "let's go home."

The three of us get back in the car.

"You okay, Champ?"

"I'm fine." I start the engine and drive out of the parking lot and onto the road to the highway. After about half a mile, I pull over, try to catch my breath.

"Anne!" Mim says from her seat beside me.

I raise my head. Look at her face. See the lines of grief and worry. "Do you want to drive, Gramps?" I ask, turning around. "I'm a little shaky."

"I'll do it." Mim exits her side. We exchange places. "Herman's been up to his old tricks. He's in no condition."

Gramps shrugs from the backseat. I give him a sweet look.

She drives down the highway. Nobody speaks on the way,

but my mind whirls like a helicopter going down. I know a secret I can't tell anyone. Not even Gramps and Mim.

When I dared look at the corpse's face back at the morgue, I did not recognize it.

Penny Caldwell was not shot in the head.

Penny Caldwell is not dead at all.

I am ready to finish the letter.

THIRTY-FOUR

HE came to the house one day when you were at school, asking if I had any odd jobs for him. Of course, I knew immediately who he was and why he had come. The man had actually cleaned himself up. He wore decent clothes, but the other-side-of-the-tracks hunger, a quality I knew well, burned in his eyes.

I stepped out on the porch and got straight to the point. "How did you find me?"

"You have good recall," he said, "real good."

"Doesn't take much memory to recognize someone who tried to kill me."

"How did I locate you after all

these years? Well now, that would be giving out information I don't want you to know, wouldn't it?" He looked around me into the house. "Quite a big place," he said, almost to himself. "Yes indeed."

"How much?" I asked. "What will it take to keep you quiet and make you disappear for good?"

He smiled, and I thought, Bastard. He has no idea what he's up against.

"I figure you love my girl," he said, leaning against the porch rail, "and don't want to lose her. She's special, has all sorts of academic accomplishments to her credit. Musical, too. Who would have thought any girl of mine had music in her?"

"You dare to have spied on her? How did you—"

"She's my child. I have rights."

"How much do you want?"

"You've done a real good job with my Maryann, Ms. Stillman, and I trust you'd like to keep her with you."

"You couldn't take her now. She wouldn't go no matter what you said."

He walked right past me into my house and picked up one of my most expensive paperweights, a clear glass orb with a monarch butterfly embedded in the middle. He held it to the light.

"Who says I want to take her from someone who raised her good? What kind of father would I be, hmm?"

"What do you want?" I walked over and took the paperweight from his hand. I put it back on the shelf. "Tell me."

"Hold on, I'm not through yet," he said, obviously enjoying himself, like a wolf closing in for the kill. "I figure I've lost a lot of tax deductions over the years due to Maryann's absence. Then there's the potential of her future. I figure she'd be the type to take care of her dad in his old age, with her kind of connections and all. Now, I'll miss that, seeing she has no knowledge of my existence, but I can live with it, provided I'm treated right. If that's not the case and you do not cooperate, I have no choice but to turn you in." He stepped close to me and put the same waxy finger in my face. "You kidnapped my girl," he whispered, "and caused the death of my wife. What's that worth, Ms. Stillman?"

Until that moment I had no fear, thinking that I had enough to buy him off, get rid of him fast, that he had no idea how much I was worth. However, I realized then he was both smart and dangerous and in no hurry to grab. He enjoyed our parley, much as a cat would play with a wounded bird. The same malicious degree of con as the cons I worked with, he had to be stopped with more than a payoff. In the meantime, I would stall.

"How much?" I asked for the last time.

He grinned, sat down on the couch, crossed one leg over the other. "Let's start the bidding at a mil, shall we?" he asked. "Do I hear one-point-one?"

THIRTY-FIVE

BIANCA enters my room. I look at the remaining paragraphs of Mom's confession and fold over the pages. I force a smile. "I didn't hear you."

"What are you reading?"

"Instructions for my mother's burial." I walk to the dresser. Slide the letter in the top drawer. If only I could tell her!

"Looks like she really thought a lot about, you know, her—"

"Death? Yeah. The funeral's next week. It's private. We're going to send her on her way quietly."

Bianca sits on my bed. "I don't mean to be insensitive, but you sound a little cold about the whole thing. You're not repressing your feelings, are you? It could give you an ulcer."

"I'll be all right."

"Is it okay if my mother and I attend the service?"

"We're holding it at Manning's Funeral Home, Thursday

at ten. I don't know whether to put an announcement in the paper. Practically no one in town knows her."

"I hope there's not going to be an open casket. Okay, I just won't look."

"My mother will be cremated, so all you'll see is an urn full of ashes."

Bianca makes a face. "Do you know how gross that sounds? Are you sure you're not going all weird?" She stares at me from where she sits.

I wait, but she doesn't speak for several minutes. I go to my desk and pretend to arrange papers.

"Okay," she says, getting up, "I have a theory."

"You always do."

"Do you think I haven't noticed the change in you?" she asks. "Your mom has passed away, but you're so cool about it now. I think of how crazy you got when you thought she was missing in the first place. Now, for at least three weeks you've been avoiding me—me, your best friend." She puts her hands on her hips. "Something is going on, and you're not talking."

"You and your imagination." I turn away, wondering how she got so smart about human nature.

"Annie, you're easier to read than a Dr. Seuss book. Is it still Tal the Terrible?"

"Don't mention him," I say. "I can kick myself for trusting him. I called Westfield High. He never was a student there."

"Nuh-uh!"

"Maybe he and his family were members of that gypsy cult that travels around taking everything they can get."

"Yeah, and the blonde's his cousin." We both laugh. "But Annie, it's what you're not telling me that's important. I mean, we've shared everything since junior high. Think about it. If you're in trouble—and I swear I'm right—won't you let me help? I feel useless when I see you in school or here looking sad, sometimes scared."

What a temptation to tell her everything! But I can't. Not knowing the end of Penny Caldwell's story, I do not want to drag Bianca into it.

"People are talking." She looks down at her hands.

"About what?"

"They think your mother might have been involved in something shady."

"Oh," I say, slipping on my shoes. "Small-town gossip."

"Annie, the rumors have been going around for years. The lady in the big stone house. Why is she so mysterious? What has she done? Woo-o-o!"

My face goes red. "Look, Bianca, I have to see the lawyer now about the will and everything. Want me to drop you at home on my way?"

Owen Elling's office sits between Comfort Inn and the Centerville fire department on a large lot with two small maple trees on each side of the building and a brick walkway straight up the middle. I park on the street. Walk to the door through a misty rain.

I look around the empty waiting room.

"I thought I heard a voice in the wilderness." A thin, casually dressed older man with thick white hair walks through a door. "Anne Caldwell?" I nod. "Come on back," he says, holding the door for me, "and we'll chat."

Okay, I'm prejudiced. I don't trust men who say "chat."

His office is the neatest, most organized place I've ever been in. Every item on his shelves is labeled and color coded.

Not one item sits on his desk. Not even a gum wrapper in the wastebasket. No wonder my mother chose him.

He points to a chair. "First, let me say how sorry I am. Losing a parent is hard."

"It is. Thank you."

"Have you read Penny's will?" he asks when we're seated. He takes several folders from a desk drawer and lays them out on his desk, inching them up, down, and sideways until each is the same distance from the others.

"Once."

"Then you realize your mother leaves a large estate, much more extensive than you probably know."

"From what I saw, it looked almost obscene."

"Oh, well, I don't know about that." He chuckles and opens one of the folders. "This one concerns land," he says, "land with gas leases. The one here contains stocks, bonds, and bank accounts, some overseas. The final grouping"—he opens the folder—"has the deeds to both the houses, yours and your grandparents'."

I thought Mim and Gramps had bought theirs themselves. "Will it be long before I take possession?"

I see an eyebrow rise. He clears his throat. "Your mother set up a family trust to protect some of the assets from probate. However, since her estate is so extensive, there will be taxes on some of it. So count on at least a month until I can clear all of it up. That is, if you want to retain me as your lawyer."

"You're the only one I know," I say. "By the way, every two weeks an amount is automatically transferred to my bank account."

"Yes," Elling says, "I am aware of that."

"This month there wasn't a deposit. Could you check that for me, or should I do it myself? I don't know where the money comes from. I've got enough right now, but if I have to start paying utility bills—"

"I'll take care of it." He stands up. "And you'll be informed when all of your assets are ready for you. Do you have any questions?"

"How much do you know about my mother?"

Owen Elling stumbles over his words. "Know about her? What do you mean? I take care of her legal affairs."

"Don't people tell lawyers their secrets?"

"I suppose some do, but that doesn't mean your mother had them."

"Okay," I say, smiling, "I'll wait for your call." I put out my hand, and he returns a half smile while shaking it.

As I leave, I realize one thing: His reaction tells me he knows plenty about my mother. Maybe everything. And like me, he isn't talking.

THIRTY-SIX

AFTER school the next day, I drive to my bank to use the ATM. I've run out of cash except for about two hundred left over from the thousand-dollar bill. Then I'll go to First Trust to look inside the safety-deposit box. Penny's paid-up cremation certificate is in there, but what will I do with it? I can't have the funeral home cremate some unknown woman's body.

The ATM eats my card.

In the lobby, I wait in line for a teller. She calls the manager. He motions me to his cubicle.

"Your funds have been frozen," he says.

"What do you mean?"

"I suggest you see your lawyer."

I stare at him.

"I can't give out information, you know."

"But it's my account."

"Please, Ms. Caldwell."

I screech out of the parking lot toward the north side of town and First Trust.

The bank officer tells me, "You have been denied access to the box at this time."

I dial Owen Elling.

"Mr. Elling is out of the office," a female voice says.

"Tell him to call me, please?" I say. "It's important." I give my cell number.

Outside the bank, I sit in my car wondering what to do. Mim will be worried about me. I have to go home.

In my room, I sort through the remaining recordings. Will anything come of spending so much time on them? From my dresser drawer I take out the letter. See that Penny signed it and even had it notarized at the bottom of the last page.

```
It didn't take me long to pull out one
of my big guns, not literally, but my
ace of spades to quash any hope this
man had of conning money from me. Oh
yes, I would have paid to get rid of
him. But he wanted too much, and I
saw it in the way his eyes toured the
room that he would never stop haunt-
ing me.
    "Listen," I told his smug face, "you
are going to leave now. I have infor-
mation that proves you have no blood
ties to my daughter. Have you seen the
copy of her birth certificate?"
```

"The real one or the one you had made up special?"

"I didn't have to fabricate one," I said. "A little research in Springfield told me everything I needed to know. Let's see, father: unknown. My, my. Had the two of you split up by then? My guess is that you ran off from your responsibilities for a while, then came back after your wife had conceived, given birth, and given me the child. But eventually, you caught on to her scam, and when she refused to share her profits with you, why, I suspect you might have done something, shall we say, criminal to her? Do you think for a second I believed the heart attack story?"

For a moment, I thought the man was going to kill me. I kept my finger on the 911 button of my cell in my pants pocket. But he stood and looked toward the door. "I am that little girl's father," he said, not quite as confidently as before.

"Then you'll have to prove it by taking, in my presence, a blood test. Today I think it's done with a swab to the mouth. If it shows without question you are the father, I will gladly give you a settlement."

Whatever education this man lacked, he understood perfectly when it came to paternity tests. He knew his golden goose was killed and cooked, with only the carcass left. I showed him the door and never heard from him again.

It was a lucky guess. I had done no research, found no birth certificate. At the time, there were only my observations of a woman with a horde of children and no regular man anywhere on the premises. By some strange spark of memory, I recalled her name, though I didn't think I knew it at the time you came to me wrapped in a blanket. That day I was so flabbergasted by my "gift," nothing registered, but a few years ago while looking through some of your baby pictures, I saw in my mind a name on a row of mailboxes where your family lived: "Eleanor," as plain as anything, "Eleanor" something. You are the daughter of Eleanor, and your first name is Maryann. For the life of me, though, I cannot remember her last name. All I know is the man who said he was your father and Eleanor did not share it.

Beware of this lowlife, Anne. He could return someday. Believe me, once someone like him works his way into your life, you can never close the door because he's stuck his dirty foot permanently in the opening. His name is Dill Smith, I found out, and he may have been the common-law husband of your birth mother. That's all I know, but it shouldn't be too hard to find out.

Now, my sweetness, you know almost everything about your life and mine. May you understand that what I've done has been to protect you, though also from my desire to do something special, something risky and exciting. That need has its downside, too. Because you're reading this letter, one of several things has happened. I am

- incarcerated somewhere out of the country.
- hiding from my employers, who have decided they have no further use for me.
- dead (my employers have probably found me).
- dead (someone else has found me).

Now that I am gone, please contact Owen Elling, and, Anne, keep your eyes wide open as you examine items at the house and handle my affairs. Sell nothing, throw nothing out, give nothing away. Eventually, you will find what waits for you. Think hard. I know you can.

```
      Upon my death, Owen Elling has power
of attorney. The document is at his
office.

                          All my love,
                          Mom


  Signed, Penny Caldwell, August 20, 2007
                      Notary: Owen Elling
                     Witness: Joyce Elling
```

I look again at the list of reasons. First of all, she isn't dead. She's not in another country. It doesn't make sense that someone in a foreign country would fake her death and send a body to Centerville. Maybe she's in hiding. But how did she set up her "death"? Who helped her? Owen Elling? Probably not, but I can't rule that out. Could Penny be missing for another reason?

I try Elling's office again. "Did you contact him about me?" I ask. "It's an emergency."

"He's not answering his messages," the woman says.

If I don't hear from Elling soon, I'll try to find out myself why my bank account has been frozen.

THIRTY-SEVEN

NEXT day I make a list of to-dos. I tell Mim and Gramps not to worry because I have a band rehearsal after school for an upcoming concert. I don't like lying to them. Before leaving campus, I ask Bianca to meet me at my house Saturday morning. Eight sharp.

"That's early," she whines. "What's up?"

"Don't ask," I say. "You wanted to help, and now you can."

"Oh, fun. We're going to clean up the place, huh?"

"Yes, I do so hope to clean up."

After school in the parking lot as I unlock my Jeep, I hear someone behind me.

I turn and see Junior, arms folded over his chest. His right foot taps the asphalt. I open the door.

"Wait," he says, "I have something for you."

I throw my backpack onto the shotgun seat and start to get in. He grabs my arm and pulls me upright. I twist away.

"Hold on. Someone wants to meet with you tomorrow afternoon."

"Who?"

Junior shrugs. "The message came today after math, but you'd already left. I saw it on the teacher's desk, so I picked it up. Here."

He digs in one pocket and hands me a wrinkled envelope with my name and URGENT on the front. I take out a sheet of paper with a typed note.

> *Anne, go alone to the coffee shop at Redman's Motel*
> *Saturday afternoon. Arrive at four-thirty and wait.*

I give Junior a look. "You opened it."

"The 'urgent' part made me curious. I can drive out there with you if you're scared, protect you, be the man now that Tal's gone. Where is he anyway?"

"Are you sure you didn't write this to mess with me?" I slide past him into the driver's seat and close the door.

"Don't thank me or anything," he calls as I start the engine and back out of the parking space.

Who will be waiting for me at Redman's? Is Junior amusing himself? What about J.J.? I read that mobsters carry out hits in public places. Why not in Centerville? At the moment, it's on to Owen Elling's office.

When I arrive, one car is in the lot.

"Mr. Elling still hasn't come in." A middle-aged woman with a sleepy face sits behind a desk. "I told you yesterday I'll give him your message."

"Have you talked with him at all since I called?" I look past her to his office door, which is slightly open.

"Of course," she says, "but he's very busy with an emergency out of town. I don't know when he'll be able to call you."

I thank her and leave. Instead of getting into my car, I walk around the rear of the building. There, by the door, I see a dark blue Escalade with the back open. Staying out of sight, I wait. Soon the receptionist comes out the door carrying a file box, followed by Owen Elling with two more. They put them in the vehicle. Elling shuts the hatch.

"Maybe you should call her," the woman says. "After all, she's Penny's daughter."

"Not now." He pulls keys from his pocket. "You know what to say if she comes here again." He puts an arm around her shoulders. "Take care, Joyce," he says. "Hold down the fort, and I'll check in after I arrive." He kisses her cheek.

"Be careful, dear."

Elling's wife!

I creep away to my car. Sit until I see him leave the parking lot, then turn onto the street after him. How fast can an old man go? I ask myself as we drive toward the highway. Once on it, I answer: as fast as a NASCAR driver! The man must have floored the gas pedal. I can hardly see him with the distance he has put between us. I drive as fast as I dare. My speedometer hits eighty, and the Escalade is still shrinking.

He disappears. I slap the steering wheel. Where has he gone? As I pass a gas station a couple of miles up the road, I turn my head and see the Escalade parked at a pump. I pull off and wait. Five minutes later he drives by. When I think the time is right, I start after him.

The car evaporates again, so I speed up a bit. Manage to keep the dot on the horizon. I hope he won't stay on the road too long. I look at my watch: 1:30 PM. Where is he taking those boxes? What's in them, my mother's records? Money? Maybe Owen Elling is a courier, too. Is he making a delivery?

Then I lose him.

At Middleboro, the traffic picks up. I can't keep Elling's car in sight. By the time I drive out in the country, the road is empty. He must have exited at the town. Where did he go after that?

With the car turned around, I drive back and get off at Middleboro. The place isn't big. The usual fast-food restaurants and a couple of run-down motels. I look for the business district sign. Make a right at Main Street through a residential section that eventually turns into an area with shops. I don't see the Escalade anywhere but spot a small brick library. I park and go in. Search for computers with Internet service. The only two are in use. I walk to the front desk. A bald man with a pointed beard stands behind it.

"I wonder if you could answer a question," I say.

He looks up. "Of course."

"My birth certificate. How would I find a copy if I was born in Chicago?"

"Are you eighteen yet?" I shake my head. "If you want an official copy, you can't order one until that time. As far as I know, the rule generally applies to anyone born in the U.S. Otherwise, a parent or guardian is necessary." He puts his hands on the counter and leans my way. "I only know that because my stepson needed one recently to get a job."

"If my parents are dead, and I don't know my guardian's whereabouts, then what?"

The man frowns. "Good question. Let me bring up the Illinois vital records site." He sits down at his computer, Googles the information. "Well, says here a legal representative can sign for it, or an interested person might be able to go to the recorder in his or her birth county and view the information, that is, if the particular person in charge sees a good reason to allow it." He looks at me. "Lost your birth certificate, huh?"

I shifted from one foot to the other. "I've never had one. I was adopted."

"Oh. That might give you more trouble. My, you have the prettiest color hair. I'll bet your name is Colleen."

"Yeah. How'd you know?"

He laughs. "I was joking. Get it?"

"It's Anne, actually. May I borrow your phone book?"

He hands one to me and goes back to his work. I thumb through the government pages, wondering where the nearest FBI office is. Springfield. None in Middleboro or Centerville. I copy down the address and number, also the number of the vital records office, before putting the book on the man's desk. There isn't time now to drive to Springfield.

But I can call.

"Good luck, Anne," he says.

Getting back to Centerville takes forty-five minutes. On the way, I phone Vital Records, state my name, ask if I can view my birth certificate.

"Let me look it up," says a nasal voice on the other end. "If you bring ID, there won't be a problem. But there's no certificate for an Anne Caldwell in our system."

"Oh, right!" I force a laugh. "I was adopted. My real name is Maryann, born around November 10, 1990."

"Last name?"

"I don't know, but my birth mother's name was Eleanor something."

A moment later she says, "Yes, I see it. Maybe. Actually, not the tenth. A few days earlier."

My heart speeds up. "What was my last name?"

"I can't tell you that. Not until you prove who you are."

"But I don't think I can. I just found out."

"That's our policy."

"Really?"

My voice must sound pathetic because she softens. "What I can tell you is that someone else ordered a copy of it fairly recently."

"Who!"

"I'm not authorized to say anything more. But, oh, what can it hurt? It looks like a Penny Caldwell. Your mother?"

"Yes!"

"Well, there you are. She must have it, so all you have to do is ask to see it."

My next stop is the police station. Detective Rodriguez seems glad to see me. Today she's wearing tan pants and a wool tweed jacket with little red flecks.

"How's it going, Anne?" she says, putting a hand on my shoulder. "I'm getting ready to leave. Been on duty for twelve hours."

"Am I holding you up?" I ask. "I have a question."

"I always have time for you. Sit down." She points to a chair beside her desk.

I glance around at all the desks, close together and occupied. "Could we go outside?"

"Of course."

We walk out and round the side of the building. "I've got an APB out for J.J. San Marino, a felon out of Gary," she says. "Have you heard from him again?"

"No, but he sounded serious about showing up when he threatened me."

"Try not to worry about it. We're on it."

"Okay. This is it: my mother's alive," I tell her. "The body I identified wasn't hers. The cop at the morgue told me not to say anything, but the funeral's next Tuesday, and I'm wondering what I should do about that."

"Wait a minute. You're saying the dead woman isn't your mother?"

"Well, yeah."

Detective Rodriguez frowns and stares past me. "You're positive. Who's the cop?"

"I don't know. But someone wants everyone else to think she died except me. I went along with the ID business. But what do I do now?"

"Interesting. Do you have any idea where your mother might be?"

I shake my head.

"Let me make some phone calls and get back to you tonight. I want to find out who that officer is. Still at your grandparents'?"

"Yes," I say. "But call me on my cell. They don't know about Mom."

"Right."

It's four in the afternoon, almost dark by the time I reach my street. I know nothing more than when I started out. Except that Mom got a copy of my birth certificate. Wherever it is.

After nine, Detective Rodriguez calls. I hold my breath.

"I was told point-blank not to ask questions about your mother. What did it tell me? Something important is going down. Unfortunately, I don't know what or why."

"Detective, I'm out of ideas. What should I do?"

"First, here's my cell number. Program it into yours. Call me anytime, and I mean anytime you have a question or problem. Got a pencil? 555–2888. Next, put a notice in the paper that services will be private, and make sure to include relevant statistics about your mother: birth, death, major accomplishments. Go to the funeral and take the ashes with you when you leave," she said.

"All right, but is the surrogate body going to be cremated?"

"That won't happen."

"Then what—"

"It's all I know, except the ashes in the urn will not be human."

THIRTY-EIGHT

BIANCA and I stand at the entrance of the stone house. I unlock the door and punch in the code. The policeman sits in the unmarked car in the driveway drinking coffee and looking bored enough to sleep.

She enters first, makes a 360-degree turn. "What a disaster. Where do we begin?"

"First, let's talk. Come on—sit on the couch."

"Can you turn up the heat a little? It's like a cave in here."

I go into the hallway and set the thermostat. I turn on a light and sit next to Bianca. "Before we begin, you need to know we're not cleaning up the mess. We're searching for treasure."

"Stuff your mom left here before she—"

"About a month ago, I found a whole lot of money she had hidden in a hollowed-out book. Tal took it. That's why he ran away."

"Why, that, that rotten—"

199

"Okay, okay," I say. "He's a snake, but at the time it disappeared, I didn't need it. Now I do. My bank account is frozen. I don't know why, and in a letter Mom left for me, she said she stashed cash wherever she lived, just in case. She wants me to figure out where she put it."

Bianca clears her throat. "Don't you see, Annie? If your account is frozen, that means the government, probably the IRS, has seized your money because it's dirty. We learned that in civics last year."

"Maybe, but I'm more worried about Mim and Gramps. They don't have much. I want to make sure they're okay if I'm going to stay with them. They have no clue my mom might be in trouble with the law."

"Was," Bianca says. "Hey, you all right?"

I take a deep breath. Bianca, poised at the edge of the couch, seems to know there's more, and I have to tell her. I have to tell someone. "How much do you divulge to your mother?" I ask. "If I let you in on something, are you going to, like, run right home and act like a parrot?"

"You know I won't. Come on, Annie!"

"It's tabloid stuff."

"Of course it is." She pauses. "Okay, if I tell, you can blackmail me with this tidbit: I made out with Wayne Bauer in the back of his car."

"Wayne? Ew! Why?"

"Because he was there, and I wondered what it would be like."

"And?"

"I'm entering the convent after high school."

I laughed.

"Truth? It wasn't bad. His lips were surprisingly expressive. I . . . We did it again a few more times."

I sit with my mouth open.

"It didn't last long, but now I know. So. I'm ready to listen."

For the next half hour she learns about the letter. My real background. My so-called grandparents. My mother's miraculous recovery from the dead. "But I don't know where she is or why someone shipped another deceased woman to Centerville," I say. "I think she's in serious trouble."

Bianca slumps back against the couch. "Holy crap, that's some story to lay on me so early in the morning. Get out! Your dead mom isn't dead, but she isn't your real mom anyway, who *is* dead. Your grandparents aren't your real grandparents. Is your cat your real cat?"

In Mom's room we pick over as much territory as possible. Open books. Slip our fingers along walls and the backs of pictures. Sift through shoes, books, crates, metal boxes, closet shelves, drawers. Nothing. Next, we look in her bathroom. Stocked with every type of cleaner as well as dozens of cans of deodorant, foot, and disinfectant sprays. I'm beginning to think my mother has a serious complex involving the world of microbes.

I try pulling up carpet to see if there's a vault in the floor. Wasted energy.

Kitchen: Nothing. Not in drawers, cabinets, broom closets full of more cleaning supplies. Whatever else describes Penny, Ms. Clean is right up there.

"Food. I need food," Bianca says at one-thirty. "Let's break for lunch."

"We'll have to go to Mim's or out someplace. Unless graham crackers and peanut butter will do it for you."

"Do you really think this house has money stuffed some-where?"

"Yep." I open a cupboard door and take out some beef jerky. "Hey, maybe this will hold us until later."

Bianca looks at her watch. "Oh no, I forgot! My mom has some shindig planned after my brother's Pop Warner game this afternoon. It's the little fart's birthday. She'll kill me if I don't show up. Let's try again after school Monday. In the meantime, I'll lend you some cash. How much do you need?"

I tell her I have enough for a few more days. What is she thinking? Her family has to watch every cent. She shares her earnings from the bookstore with them.

"Come with me. This place is too depressing."

"Thanks, but I'm going to look a little longer."

Soon I'm alone in the house. Why can't I locate a small stack of thousand-dollar bills? Because Mom hid all of it from scum who know where to look. She must have left me a clue. But at the moment, I only have a torn-apart house.

After scrounging through more drawers, the secret pas-sage, even the empty guest cottage, I lock up and go to my car. Call my grandparents. Tell them I'll be running errands until six, then set off for Redman's.

I arrive at three-thirty, order coffee and a chicken sand-wich, my first real food of the day. Push it around the plate when it arrives. Keep my eye on the door.

Owned by a farmer, Redman's sits a mile out of Center-ville in the middle of a cornfield now covered with snow. A two-story-high Indian-head penny, bordered with a row of flashing red lightbulbs, signals the café from the highway 24/7. Around the area, the coffee shop, with its red and white awnings in the summer, is famous for fried chicken and rhubarb pie. Inside, the booths have blond wood trim and bright red plastic upholstery covered with ranch brands. Splashy posters of wigwams, Indians, and cowboys speckled with grease cover the walls.

The light from the sky fades, leaving pale pink behind the bare trees across the highway. At four-thirty, I pick up my tab. Go to the cashier. Out of the corner of my eye, I see Owen Elling in a leather jacket carry a briefcase through the door. He glances around, spots me, hurries over.

"Thank goodness you came," he says, out of breath. He takes off his jacket, drapes it over one arm. "Come and sit down. So sorry I'm late."

"Why didn't you just call?" I ask after we choose a booth in the back. "I thought someone was playing a trick on me."

"Believe it or not, delivering an envelope to the school was safer. The phones might be bugged. I couldn't take a chance. May I order you something?"

I shake my head.

"Someone in a yellow Jeep followed me yesterday."

I pretend to read the paper place mat.

"I wonder who it could be. You have a lot of spunk, young lady. What did you hope to find by chasing me down the highway?"

Pat the waitress comes over, stands with pencil poised over ordering pad. "Our special of the day—"

"Just hot tea," he says.

When she walks away, I lean toward him. "Please tell me what's going on. Where is my mother? What happened to my bank accounts?"

"You know about Penny?"

"I identified the 'body.' "

"That wasn't supposed to happen. The local police fouled

up. No, you were to be told that the corpse had deteriorated too much and that Penny's identity would be confirmed through dental records. Later you would learn the truth."

"Maybe the body at the morgue is kept in storage for a stand-in. Like a stunt body."

Elling frowns.

"Please tell me where she is. Who's hiding her and from what?"

"I don't know everything, but here's what I came to say." He opens his briefcase and pulls out some papers. "Because I am Penny's lawyer, I was contacted. Until a few days ago, I also thought she had died. I had no idea what trouble she was in."

"Who contacted you?"

"U.S. marshals."

"Someone shut down Mom's and my accounts. I can't get into her safety-deposit box either. My grandparents' money might also be in trouble."

"No, their holdings are exempt. As for the accounts, the government seized them because of— Are you aware of her 'occupation'?"

"Yes, but I read Mom's letter, and I can't believe you didn't know. You signed it!"

Elling adjusts his tie. "Young lady, I'm a reputable attorney who would never overstep the legal system."

He looks down at the papers on the table. "You're going to lose your lifestyle as you now know it. There's not much I can do about that. I can probably salvage something, at least for you because you are the innocent one in all this. But the house and its contents will be sold and most of the accounts seized. I'm sorry."

"What will happen to the money?"

"The U.S. marshals will use it to further their criminal investigations."

"Where is my mother?"

"I don't know."

"Did you see her yesterday?"

"No, I met with a deputy U.S. marshal." He pauses as Pat puts down a cup and a pot of water in front of him. When she leaves, he pours some water over the tea bag. Stirs it. Removes the bag to the saucer. Takes a sip. "Your mother has joined the Witness Protection Program. She has been hidden away in another state with a new identity in exchange for her testimony next year at the trial of some very vicious individuals. I must do my work for you and her through marshals, not the most convenient path, but I am cooperating."

"What's going to happen to me? Why didn't she tell me she hadn't died instead of letting me think something else?" I'm close to tears but vow Elling won't see me cry.

"Penny was arrested the last time she left Centerville. The FBI gave her a choice: prison or testimony. She couldn't tell you because others would be looking for her, and the organization under investigation has unpleasant ways of dealing with relatives left behind."

"I feel abandoned on someone's doorstep."

"It must seem that way, but I've been told you have been under surveillance and protection since your mother's departure."

"No one protected me from getting robbed. What protection?"

Owen Elling clears his throat and takes another sip of tea. "Remember, at that time I also was unaware. I can only share what a deputy marshal told me. Now, these documents list what you may keep from your mother's estate. It's not much:

your vehicle, your bonds with a purchase date before the stoppage of Penny's writing payments, your checking account minus five thousand dollars."

"That leaves only about a thousand!"

He gives me a sharp look. "Better than zero, isn't it? The safety-deposit box contains nothing that interests the IRS. That will be released to you on Monday."

I look through the papers. Way different from what I saw a little more than a month ago. "Will I be able to join my mother?"

"Is that what you wish?" He lowers his voice. "I seem to detect a certain ambivalence toward her. She must feel a great deal of guilt over this unfortunate series of events. At any rate, you have a choice, Anne. If you decide to live with Penny, you may never visit Centerville again, never contact your friends or grandparents because it could cause the death of your mother, even *you* if your whereabouts become known. Would you be willing to give up these people in your life? If not, you could choose to stay here. In that case, you must never see your mother again."

I look out the window. It's black as death in the foreground, but snow drifts down around the streetlights. The on-and-off flashing of the red Indian head–penny bulbs turns a stand of trees across the field into an eerie slideshow.

Like my life. On and off.

"Mim will worry if I don't go home soon," I say.

Owen Elling rises and puts the papers back in his briefcase. "I'll keep these for now," he says. "You have some thinking to do. When you've made your decision, come to the office. Remember, don't call."

"Tell me," I say, pulling on my jacket, "what was in those boxes you took along with you yesterday?"

"Penny's old records, all the ones I've kept over the years. They must be transferred to computer. I lag a bit behind when it comes to technology. However, I'm looking out for your interests the best way I know how."

We walk outside, say good-bye, go directly to our cars. I wonder on the way back why he didn't just burn the boxes. What good are old records now? Then I remember Elling's words: "Penny's old records, all the ones I've kept over the years." And the night my mother told me he had been her lawyer "for about a year."

I take out my cell phone. "Gramps," I say as I drive into town, "I've got one more stop and then I'll be home, okay?"

"We've been worried. You told us six, and you know Mim."

I call Bianca. Or try to. I want her to meet me, help me look again, just be with me in that dark old place. Her cell is turned off, which means she's at work.

But I pull into the driveway of the big stone house anyway.

The cop car's there. No problem.

THIRTY-NINE

AS I step through the front door into the dark living room, my antenna rises. My eyes travel to the stairs, then up toward the faint light coming from one of the bedrooms. Could I have left it on this afternoon? I try to remember.

My common sense says, "Get out of here!" I look at the door. The law is right outside. I turn toward the stairs.

Slowly, I climb to the second-floor landing and pause, listening. Not a sound. I walk into Mom's room, flip on the light. Same mess. Boxes, books everywhere. Contents of drawers spilled out onto the carpet. I glance up. The bathroom door. Had I left it half closed?

I decide to go through the boxes one more time. After I turn on the lamp, I sit on the floor, take the first item off the top. My eighth-grade graduation program. Great day. Mom had treated Bianca and me to a weekend trip at Disney World, starting with a limousine ride from the school to the airport. Bianca's mom never got over that one. Next, a bunch of magazines with articles Mom had written. Various news stories she probably used for research.

I pull out an ad torn from some kind of catalog. Why did she keep worthless junk like this? I'd have plenty of garbage bags to fill before leaving the house.

End of the first box and on to the second. Same kind of stuff for the recycling bin. In the middle of the box, I pick up a copy of a similar-looking ad. Weird. Maybe Mom didn't remember she had the other one, but why did she want either in the first place?

Then I read it.

Of course.

Moving to the final box, I flip through it as fast as I can. The third ad lies near the bottom.

How clever.

I put the three pages together and tear them into tiny pieces.

Out of the corner of my eye, I see the bathroom door move. What I want is on a shelf in there. You're too paranoid, I tell myself. I stand and walk through the door. Turn on the light. Immediately I smell musk cologne and cigarettes.

A voice in a low monotone says, "So." He steps in front of me. A man dressed completely in black.

"J.J.?" I whisper.

His eyes are dark and filmy, his black hair long in back, straight. He has a high forehead, thick eyebrows and lips. "Where's Diane?

"D-dead. She's dead."

His upper lip twitches. "That so."

He moves closer. I step backward. My foot hits the shower door. "Last week outside Kansas City. She was—murdered."

"I hadn't heard."

I nod. "It's true." He's too close. A wave of panic leaves me breathless. "No one is supposed to get in here," I say. "They told me the alarm was foolproof. How did you–"

"Quiet. You're going to find something for me."

I'm dizzy. Petrified. Don't want him to know it. I edge by him into the bedroom. My lips quiver. "What do you want me to find?"

Instantly, he's six inches from my face again. Takes hold of my upper arms, squeezes hard. "I need the list," he says through clenched teeth. "Diane promised it to me as a favor. She didn't deliver." He lets go of me and snaps his fingers. "Where's the computer? I'll start with that."

"You weren't one of them?"

"What are you talking about?"

"The robbers. Can't you tell this house was ransacked?"

He glances around. Shrugs. "Maybe Bustos did it. Hand over the computer."

"They took it."

"Who?"

"The people who robbed us."

He surveys the room. "There's a duplicate somewhere. She was thorough. Where would she put things she doesn't want found?"

"I don't know anything. I came here to try to clean up the place."

"That why I heard you ripping up something?"

"Stuff Mom saved. Nothing important."

J.J. puts one finger under my chin. "You lie."

I wonder if I can outrun him.

"This house has been under surveillance," I say, trying to keep my voice steady. "There's a policeman sitting right out front."

He ignores me and prowls around the room, touching an item here and there. Stops. "I'll tell you what you're going to do," he says, coming close enough to nauseate me. He puts a hand on my neck. "You're going on a hunt, and when you find the list, which you will recognize, being the smart girl you are, as the one my associates and I desire, you will contact me immediately."

He takes a pen from his pocket, turns over my left hand, writes a number on my palm.

He'll send a friend of a friend of a friend for pickup, I think, and no one will ever be able to trace it. Because he'll kill me while he's at it.

"I can't help you. I don't know anything about my mother's business. She never talked about her work to me."

J.J. puts his head back and laughs, a deep phlegmy laugh. He coughs up something disgusting sounding and spits it on the floor. "Your mother's business. What a crock. Oh, she was good, very good at what she did. Do you know how talented she was?"

I shake my head.

"Diane could come up with the most ingenious, the most brilliant places to hide things. The best, I do believe, was in her sunglasses. A vial. Smaller than a silk thread. Absolutely undetectable in airport security. And very valuable to our friends overseas. A false tooth hollowed out. That was a good one, too. You name it. Diane could hide it. And now." He glances around the room. "You're going to find the list. It could be microscopic or as big as a book."

"Honestly, I don't know where to look." My stomach, a blob of acid, inches up into my chest.

"Twenty-four hours. If you don't have it, too bad for you." He goes toward the hall door, then stops. Takes a cigarette from his shirt pocket, lights it, inhales and holds in the smoke. He finally blows out a long plume.

I'm cemented to the spot.

J.J.'s voice is soft but without a hair of emotion. "Do you think I'm an idiot, kid? Diane's in hiding, not dead. And if you tell anyone about this, I promise both you and your mother will die."

My legs shake so hard I try pushing one knee into the other to keep him from noticing.

He stands in the doorway. Looks me over. "Don't forget," he says, "twenty-four hours." He walks back into the bedroom, close to me again. Drags his index finger across my throat. Whispers, "Or. You. Will. Be. Sorry."

He leaves. I hear his feet on the stairs, the door closing below. My feet won't move. My heart races.

Cell! I think. Get your cell! I race to my backpack and speed-dial the detective.

"Rodriguez here." The voice of God Himself could not make me happier.

"Detective, I'm at my house. J.J. was just here and threatened to kill me."

"Where's Ingals? He's supposed to be out front."

"When I came, his car was in the driveway."

"Can you describe what San Marino's wearing while I call up his mug shot?"

"Dark pants and shirt. Black clothes, hair, eyes." Soul. "Won't he be hard to see?"

"We'll find him. I'll radio officers in the vicinity for backup. Is your door locked?"

"I don't know. I heard it close when he left, but he's got the code."

"Lock the door immediately and engage the dead bolt. Don't hang up. Talk to me as you go."

I walk to the landing. "The door's still open! I swear he closed it."

"Do you see the suspect inside? Don't go down the stairs. Look briefly around."

I hiccup.

"What?"

"Nothing. I don't see him. Should I hide?" Another hiccup.

"I'm going to radio the officers now. Get in the bathroom, lock the door. Keep the light off. I'm on my way. Do not come out until you hear my voice in person, understand?"

I tell her okay. Instead of going in the bathroom, where my hiccups will echo like submarine bleeps, I hurry to the back of my mother's closet and through the secret door. I wait motionless on the staircase leading to the pantry, then inch down. Listen several steps up from the closed kitchen door.

He's in there going through the drawers. I hear the clank of silverware on the tile, a pause as J.J. picks up, possibly, Mom's expensive Italian wine-bottle opener. Or the sterling silver toothpicks. Maybe the gold-plated serving pieces. Why did she buy them in the first place? No one but Mim and Gramps and Bianca ever ate with us. Take them, I think. Take them all and get out!

Minutes pass like snails. I keep a fist crammed against my mouth to cork the hiccups while my stomach heaves up and down like a water pump. I haven't taken off my jacket. Perspiration trickles down my face and neck. He's going to hear me or see the door, I tell myself. Sooner or later, he'll notice it and open it.

His voice. He's talking to someone. I edge down to the bottom stair, close to the door.

"So here it is. She doesn't know squat about the list. We should have figured that out. Of course she's seen me. She's no dummy either. Huh-uh. Uh-huh. Upstairs where I left her." Long pause. "Okay."

Silence.

Okay, what? Okay, kill me?

He's on his way to the second floor. Did I close the door in the back of the closet? I can't remember. I have to move. Fast.

I turn the knob to the pantry and push the door open a crack. Nothing in view. A little wider. I wait half a minute, edge into the kitchen, creep toward the French doors, reach for the handle.

A noise. Feet on the carpet. He's coming back down the stairs! I don't have time to go into the pantry again, so I duck behind the counter next to the designer metal trash can.

"Little Red Riding Hood," he says in his monotone, about five feet from where I crouch. "Come to J.J."

Don't hiccup. Don't you dare! I tell myself.

"Get in here." J.J.'s head rises over the counter. I see him, but he doesn't see me.

His eyes narrow. "We need to talk." He walks into the living room. "Where are you?" Then he comes back into the kitchen. Stands at the sink looking around.

He turns. His eyes find me. He saw me in the reflection in the window over the sink! One corner of his mouth twitches into a half smile. Then he walks toward me slowly around the trash can. With a scarf in both hands.

All the better to strangle you with, my dear.

I roll on my back, and as hard as I can, jam the trash can into his knees with my feet. He falls against the stove and slides to the floor, groaning and cussing.

I get up and run past him, out the French doors.

Police cars come up the driveway.

I drop down behind a tree and try to breathe.

FORTY

DETECTIVE Rodriguez finishes filling out her report at the kitchen table. I lean against the counter, looking at the trash all over the floor. The police have hauled J.J. away. I still have the hiccups.

"I'm so psyched you caught him," I say.

"*We* caught him?" She stands and puts a hand on her hip, shakes her head. "Those are some weapons you used: feet and a trash can." She rolls her eyes. "Stay away from here from now on. It's not safe, apparently, even with surveillance, since Mr. San Marino knocked out Ingals, took the key and code, and left him tied up in the car. Come on. I'll follow you to your grandparents'." She slips on her coat. "Am I beat."

"Yeah, me too. This dump. I've got to do something about it."

"Forget it. Keep out." The detective thinks for a moment. "Do you believe J.J. is the man who molested you during the robbery? According to his rap sheet, it's not one of his MOs, but I have to ask."

The memory of that night makes me shudder. "No. I'm sure he didn't. I mentioned the robbery tonight. He seemed surprised. Besides, he reeks. I'd remember that."

"We won't rule him out." She gives me a weary smile. "I want your word you'll stay out of this house."

"Okay."

"No 'okay'! Your word. I got notice that we don't have the manpower to continue surveillance after tonight, especially now that the suspect is in custody. We'll do drive-bys, but that's all. I don't want you in here for any reason."

How can I give my word when I know? Those ads I tore up told me exactly where my mother hid the money. For now, I'll have to make sure the house is locked tighter than a vault and wait. I trust Detective Rodriguez, but I have to keep what I discovered to myself.

"I promise, Detective."

After I deliver Gramps and Mim a watered-down version of the J.J. incident, which shocks them enough, the hiccups start up again. Mim makes me breathe into a paper bag, then take a drink of water while keeping a pencil between my nose and upper lip. I don't know why it works, but it always does.

I'm too tired to eat. So I shower and get ready for bed. I remember both Tal's and the detective's warnings to be careful. My visit to the house tonight could have turned out much worse with Officer Ingals out of commission. But at least I can forget the list.

• • •

Next morning Gramps and Mim go off to church. They aren't exactly regulars, but maybe they think they should thank God I'm still alive. The rest of the day I lie around. Let my thoughts go where they want about Mom, J.J., Tal, Elling, Evan. "Mom, please be safe," I say.

At one point I take out my cell, bring up the photo Tal's mom took of Tal and me the afternoon we celebrated my birthday. I look at others of Tal. Delete all but the photo of the two of us. One of Tal's hands rests on my shoulder. I remember how warm it felt. The other is in his pocket. Big grin. My hair all windblown and crazy. I'm happy. Seems long ago.

I walk around the bedroom. Decide to clean it up to take my mind off sad memories. I pull open the top dresser drawer, see Mom's tapes. I've heard them all except the one from Mom's desk. Where is it? I dump the contents of my backpack on the bed. It drops out in the middle of pens and loose change.

Why not listen to it? I put everything into the backpack again, slip the tape into the player. I plug in the earphones, lean back against the bed pillows, take a deep breath. Mom. I miss that voice with the little laugh! She asks a question. A man speaks. Race-car driver. How he got started, his victories. His voice drones on. No wonder people like him needed Mom. Nothing interesting on this tape. I close my eyes.

They fly open.

"Constantine Agnos, Enrique Bustos, Eddie Carbino, Bruno Evangelica, William T. Johnson, Ricardo E. Zambino."

Names, all kinds of names that go on, one after the other, for the next fifteen minutes. Each followed by cities, letters, numbers, other words I've never heard. Each pronounced by my mother in a voice I don't know.

Don't want to know.

I sit up. This has to be the list J.J. was looking for in some kind of code. Then the list stops. The race-car driver resumes with a description of his first win at Daytona.

I eject the tape and carry it out back after I grab a book of matches from the key drawer. It takes a few of them and several minutes to burn and drop what's left into the garbage bin.

Monday morning I call the newspaper and read the obituary to an employee:

PENNY CALDWELL MET AN UNTIMELY DEATH IN NOVEMBER 2007. BORN IN CHICAGO, ILLINOIS, IN 1966, MS. CALDWELL WAS A FREELANCE GHOSTWRITER MOST OF HER LIFE. SURVIVING ARE HER PARENTS, HERMAN AND MIRIAM CALDWELL, AND HER DAUGHTER, ANNE CALDWELL. SERVICES WILL BE PRIVATE.

Instead of heading for school, I drive down the highway. On the way I call the attendance office and tell the clerk I'm staying home with a headache. "Feel better," she says. I'm turning into such a slacker.

In forty-five minutes, I pull up to the FBI building in Springfield and walk in.

A man at the front desk asks if he can help me. "Are you an agent?" I ask.

"No. What is this about?"

"Bank accounts. They're frozen. My mom disappeared, and her lawyer says the IRS seized the money, but—"

"We rarely handle matters like that."

"But if someone could, well, check on things?"

The man looks sharply at me, maybe trying to decide if

I'm some kid trying to cause trouble. "All right," he says, "I'll call someone." He punches a few buttons and talks into a receiver. Hangs up and points. "Go through that door."

I walk in. A blonde with her head down sits writing at a desk. I clear my throat. She looks up.

I step back. It can't be.

The woman is Shelley Cook.

FORTY-ONE

"I know you," I say. "You were with Tal. At the mall. In Centerville. Shelley, right?"

She's wearing a suit, and her hair is shorter, but it's Shelley. I know it is. Just because I saw her once doesn't mean she saw me, though. Or even knows about me.

She smiles. Pretty. I don't blame Tal. She points to a nameplate on the desk with GWEN PIERCE in block letters. "Agent Pierce. I'm sorry, what's your name?"

"Anne Caldwell."

I saw her from across the courtyard that day. Up close, she's older. Maybe in her late twenties. I could be wrong.

She folds her hands and taps two fingers together. "People tell me constantly that I look like someone they know. So, how can I help you today?"

I take a deep breath. "Penny Caldwell, my mom, disappeared a while ago. We thought she was dead, but she's not. She's still missing. Anyway, she left me a lot of money. But when I tried to get into my bank account, the manager said the funds were frozen, and since then, I found out from my lawyer that the government has seized my account and most of my mother's money and our house, too."

She looks sympathetic. "The IRS does that, yes," she says. "It usually indicates the money was obtained illegally. Your mother's lawyer can explain why in more detail if that's what you want." She pauses, but I can't think of anything to say. She gets up. "I have an appointment soon. I don't know what else I can tell you."

"It might not mean anything," I say, "but Owen Elling—that's Mom's lawyer—lied. He said he kept her records over the years, but my mom told me before she disappeared that he had only worked for her for one year. I also saw him taking some boxes to Middleboro a few days ago. He said they were Mom's old records. Why would he do that?"

Agent Pierce thinks, walks around her desk to the door and opens it. "Do you have your bank account number with you?"

I say yes and reach in my backpack for a check.

"I'll borrow that. Wait out there until I make a couple of calls and get back to you."

In the lobby I stand and look out the window. A cold, gloomy day. No snow, only dead grass and gray cement.

I rub my eyes. It would be so easy to curl up in a chair and go to sleep. I don't want to think. I'm tired of worrying and digging around for money. What good is money anyway when you don't have a life? It's not suddenly going to get you one.

Agent Pierce returns a few minutes later. Sits next to me. "Anne," she says, "nothing of yours has been seized by the government, not your accounts, not your house. There's no record of it in our system."

"Then what—"

"I called your bank. Seems that your lawyer, using his power of attorney, told the manager you were temporarily incapable of handling money and that he would manage all transactions for the time being. You might be right about him. You can be sure we will be contacting Mr. Elling. Today."

What a scumbag. I get up. "My cell number's on my check. Or, if you have any news, you could call Detective Rodriguez at the Centerville police station. She's trying to help me find my mother."

Agent Pierce looks as if she's about to say something, then puts out her hand and pats my shoulder. "Good tip today, Anne. Nice work. I'm glad you came to us. Mr. Elling probably never dreamed you would act. Is this a school holiday?"

"No." I make a guilty face. "I'd better catch my afternoon classes."

"Yes, life goes on," Agent Pierce says.

I look at her again carefully, then shrug. "Guess you're not who I thought you were," I say, "but I could have sworn you were Tal's old girlfriend. It's crazy, but you have an exact double out there somewhere."

"I don't know anyone named Tal," she says. "Good-bye, Anne. Please call if you need anything else."

Next morning, as I drive toward my house on the way to school and think about the previous day, I squint. It can't be! I slow up and stop. Evan stands in the driveway. He wears a stained gold jacket, much too big for him, and a brown knit cap that hides his hair and half of his face like a hood. I let out a yell and wave. He comes to the Jeep, gets in.

"Hey," I say, "how's it going?"

"Okay." He blows on his hands. "You?"

"It's so good to see you!" I hug him. "Where have you been? Are you getting enough to eat, somewhere to sleep?"

"I'm fine. How's Zor Boy?"

"He misses you."

"Yeah." He looks at his hands. "Haven't been to school lately. Guess you noticed. I'm not going back. Gonna get a job somewhere or maybe go someplace warm. Anyways, I was thinking I could help you. That's why I came to your house, you know, to see if you'd drive by so I could offer to pick up the place."

I'm puzzled. "That's nice of you," I say, "but I don't have time myself to work on it, especially this week."

"I heard about your mother. I'm real sorry. I remember when my ma died. Sort of. Hit and run. No one ever found out who did it. It's hard, no matter what opinion you have of a parent."

"Thanks. Right now I need to get through semester tests. My work has so gone downhill." I put a hand on his sleeve. "I have to go. Why don't we meet later? Come over to my grandparents'. Mim will feed you something good."

"No way. That lady doesn't like me." He fools with his cap. Seems nervous. "I was thinking I could get a start in the house. I'd pick up and clean up things, and then you could tell me later what to do next. You don't have to help at all."

I hesitate. "Actually, no one's supposed to go in there. It's still a crime scene. I admit I've been in a couple of times, but for you to be there alone—what if the police stop by and arrest you for trespassing?"

"They wouldn't catch me. I know how to slip out."

I shake my head.

"Why not?"

I don't answer. We're both quiet. The snow drifts down and sticks to the windshield.

Evan breaks the silence. "I haven't been able to pay you back. You were good to me. I want to do something."

"Detective Rodriguez made me promise to stay out, and I will. Don't feel obligated, please, Evan."

"You don't even have to go in. Unlock the door, and I'll have everything nice for you by this afternoon."

"Cleaning up the place will take at least a week." I put both my hands on the steering wheel. "I have to get to school."

"Anne."

"No."

He doesn't move. I turn. Something odd shines in his eyes. Is it fear? A feeling I can't understand comes over me. Like sliding down a hill backward into a ravine.

I start the Jeep. Evan doesn't move.

"Come on, I'll be late."

He leans toward me. "I got to do it, Anne, I just got to."

"God, Evan, what's wrong with you?"

"Let me. Just this once, okay?"

I know I shouldn't. But I say, "All right, if you want to help that much. I think there's some soup in the cupboard. I'll come by after school and reset the alarm."

I put the Jeep in park, and we go up the driveway to the house. I unlock the door. Disarm the alarm. "There," I say. "Enter at your own risk. See you later. Meet me outside this door, three-thirty sharp."

Evan walks through the entrance and turns. His smile is only a shadow as he waves good-bye.

FORTY-TWO

"SO, how'd it go Saturday? Did you see Tal? He was the one who showed up, right?"

Junior hurries down the hall after me. I nearly run to avoid him. "It wasn't Tal." I push the door wide open. Scoot out.

"Hey, wait! I'm not poison. What's wrong with me, huh?"

"I stay away from guys who punch my friends."

"Jones? He gave me the finger. No one does that."

"Grow up." I walk off toward the parking lot.

"You're hot, you know?" he calls. Then whistles. "Tal thought so, too."

Wait a minute! I didn't remember the two of them ever together. But they must have been. Junior. He had to be the other one! He and Tal robbed my house. Junior tried to get what he wanted since I embarrassed him by turning him down last year.

Why hadn't I seen that? The incident with Evan in the parking lot had been a setup so that when the robbery took

place, no one could connect them as a team. During the robbery, Junior put his dirty hands all over me. Tal stopped him,
then waited for a chance to run off with my money.

It makes perfect sense. If only I had proof.

Near the end of lunch, I phone Detective Rodriguez and
tell her about the FBI and Elling. "Agent Pierce might call
you sometime," I say. "I gave her your number."

She lets out a disgusted sound. "Elling must have viewed
Penny as a cash cow after her disappearance. The rate you're
going, you'll find out where your mother is all by yourself."

I call Mim and tell her I'm on my way but will be half an
hour late. A plan comes to me as I drive up to the stone house
to set the alarm. I can pay Evan for his work, now that I'll
have access to my account. Offer him a place to stay again.
He can be my watchman. Sound the gong if someone shows
up. Truth: I don't want Evan to leave Centerville at all. I have
to give him a reason to stay.

I pull in the driveway and up to the house. During the
day, the snow has covered the lawn and bushes and apple
trees. It sticks to the stone. The porch is completely white.

Three-thirty-two. No Evan.

I let the Jeep run and flip through radio stations. Turn off
the ignition. Sit.

Three-forty.

I get out of the Jeep, walk up to the door. Push the bell.

No response. I look around.

Silence.

I try the handle. Unlocked. I enter, reset the security code.
Close the door. Stand inside. I'll be out in five minutes.

The house is dark. Silent. Cold.

I shout, "Evan! Where are you? You left the door un-locked."

Strange, I expect that at least the living room will be picked up, but if anything, it's worse.

A slight noise causes me to look up to the landing at the top of the stairs. A man stands there smiling down at me, a man I've seen only once. But I know who he is.

"Well, I swan! Penny's daughter. What does she call you—Anne? That's close, very close." He walks to the stairs. Descends slowly. One of the kind who has lines in his face that make him appear older than he is, Dill Smith wears a sleeve-less undershirt and rumpled tan cargo pants. The house can't be much more than forty degrees. He is slim, muscular, short. His arms and shoulders bulge with tattoos that spread out like black and blue fire toward his neck. A snake juts out from the top of his shirt, curves toward the back of his neck, its head just below his hair, which curls in greasy clumps around his face. That face with slits for eyes.

"Evan?" My voice comes out scared like a little girl's. "What have you done to Evan?"

The man walks to me and folds his arms against his chest. "Your mama withheld from me," he says. "She owes me money, and I need it to take care of my family and debts. I know she's got plenty, and now that you're an orphan—I'd like to say I'm sorry, but that'd be a lie—you have more than enough to share with your old daddy. That's right, surprise! I'm your daddy. Come on, give Dad a nice, big hug." He holds out his arms. The slits of his eyes open. I see the black stones of my nightmare.

"You're not my father."

The slap across my face happens so fast it knocks me backward. My head hits the arm of the couch.

"You do not talk back," the man says. "Get up."

I moan and roll over. He kicks my side hard. Something cracks. I scream.

"Get up." He stands, one foot on each side of me.

I manage to stand, so frightened I can't cry. "I don't have any money," I say. "The accounts are gone. The government seized them. This house is going to be sold—"

The next blow is a punch near the bridge of my nose. I wake up to cold water hitting my face. I choke on it, try to catch my breath. I open my eyes a little. He looks enormous standing over me. A skull on his forearm grins at me. Of all the people Penny Caldwell was involved with—con men, Feds, losers in her past—this one has to be the most dangerous.

My mother's warning was right on.

"Girl as smart as you knows where her mama hides money. You're going to tell me. I got plenty of time." He reaches down, yanks me upright. I stifle a cry. He grabs my hair and starts for the stairs.

"Are you hurting me because Eleanor had me with another man? Well, she's dead, so what good does it do to beat me up?"

He holds me rigid in front of him. I see rage in his black stone eyes. Abruptly, he punches my stomach. I throw up, and he slaps my mouth twice, hard. I taste blood. Choke on it. He continues upstairs, pulling me by the hair. I try to think beyond the next attack about what to do. The only image I see is a gravestone with my name on it.

I know where the money is. Should I risk my life for it? Or will he kill me anyway? Easy answer. My candle is about to burn out either way. I throw up again over the banister and wipe blood and vomit from my mouth.

He drags me into my mom's room. "Now, where is it? Most morons hide their cash in bedrooms. I been looking all day but haven't come acrost it. Where's the safe? The hidden panel? Come on, girl." I look at him with a blank face. I can't move or speak. Almost raising me off the floor, he throws me against the wall. I fall over the boxes I've looked through. The cardboard of one slices through my arm. I watch blood ooze toward my wrist.

He screams, "Stop stalling! Get up!"

I rise carefully, pain everywhere. "I don't know any-thing—"

His fist knocks me on top of the bed. I turn my head. Mom's white satin duvet is turning scarlet.

"Go in there, in the bathroom." The words come out slurred. "Look for the foot powder in the medicine chest."

"Stop talking nonsense." He closes in on me to beat me again.

I try to make it come out right. My jaw. Something's wrong with it. "Can of foot powder. Unscrew the bottom. Money there."

"You making fun of me?" He takes a bunch of my hair and yanks hard. "Better not be joking."

"Not. I—I'm not."

He lets go. Walks through the door. I see him open the cabinet, pull out the can. Turn it over. Unscrew the bottom. It's in there, a roll of cash. After all, the ads said, "Will hide up to $10,000 per can in $100 bills, or a lesser amount, de-pending upon the denomination."

"Hot damn!" I watch as he counts the money.

I edge off the bed, slip into Mom's closet, to the back and through the hidden door. Close it quietly. Creep down the stairs to the kitchen. The pain is horrible. I panic. Escaping out the French doors will set off the alarm. I'll have to make it to the front door and the keypad.

For sure my rib is broken, maybe my nose. I've never hurt so much, but at the same time something inside makes me run like crazy. I think it's called self-preservation. The massive oak door is in sight. I sprint as fast as I can, then trip over one of the objects scattered around the living room. I fall and knock the wind out of myself. Roll over. Struggle to get up. His hand is there again, grabbing my hair. This time he drags me across the floor. The pain is terrible.

"Stop it! Stop!" I hit at him and scream with everything I've got. A thumping comes from below.

He pauses. "I decide what you will do, not vice versa. We're going upstairs again. Git!"

I don't know how I make it up to the landing. My nose prickles in the back. A signal I'm close to blacking out. I fight it. At the top of the stairs, instead of my mother's room, he pushes me into mine and onto the bed. "Bad girls must be punished," he says. "Take off your clothes."

"You," I whisper between sobs. "You—robbed—us—that—night."

"I said, get those clothes off."

"I thought you were my daddy. Daddies—don't—they don't—"

"Shut up!" He comes at me, grabs the waist of my pants. I hear the ripping, and my eyes fill with tears.

Behind him I see a silver blur rising like a pendulum. I push myself up. Dill Smith slides to his knees in slow motion and down beside the bed. Blood from his head spreads out over the carpet like watercolor on wet paper.

Evan stands motionless, holding a shovel. "I'm sorry, Anne. Oh God, I'm so sorry!"

FORTY-THREE

WHEN the EMS rolls me into the emergency ward, the nurse who took care of me before runs over. "Well, look who's back," she says. "Not having a very good year, are you, hon?"

I'm welcomed by all of the personnel. They spoil me rotten during my three-week stay. Finishing the semester at Lincoln is not going to happen. I don't worry about it. Maybe it's the drugs.

I lose my spleen. My broken jaw has to be wired shut. Two of my ribs are taped. A plastic surgeon from Springfield rescues my nose. My black eyes change color so many times one nurse calls me Aurora Borealis. The hair loss leaves a few bald patches. "Don't worry. Hair grows back," Gramps says, "except for mine."

Detective Rodriguez is one of my first visitors after Mim and Gramps, who arrived as I was brought in. I can't even describe their sobs. For someone not even related to them, I've caused them a dump truck–ful of misery.

"Will you attend the funeral Thursday and pick up the ashes?" I ask them through a haze. "I'm not going to make it."

"Look at the snow come down." Detective Rodriguez points at the window. "You're lucky you don't have to go out in it. We're in for a cold winter."

"Yeah," I say through my teeth.

"Your injuries could have been avoided," she says with a direct look, "if you had just stayed out of the house and left the investigating to us and the FBI. But let's hear what happened in as much detail as possible, if you're well enough to do it."

"Better sit down," I say. "It's going to take a long time."

"You're probably not going to like my saying this," the detective says, "but you still could be in danger. I suspect, too, that Mr. Smith would have killed you had Evan not stopped him."

Why do the police always refer to evil people as "mister"?

Dill Smith has survived despite a large gash on the head. He's been carted off to a hospital in another town. Detective Rodriguez assures me the man has so many shackles on him he can't move an eyelash. When he recovers, he'll be locked up in the most secure prison in Illinois while awaiting trial.

"I think he killed his common-law wife in Chicago," I tell her. "Something Evan told me. Maybe you could look into it."

"I'll pass it on. Oh yes," she adds, "I found a sizable

amount of cash on him and assume it belongs to you. We're holding it at the station."

I thank her. No wonder Mom always insisted that we clean our own house. She kept the fake cleaning products inventoried and labeled because she had put cash in oven-cleaner cans, counter-cleaner cans, hair spray cans, and all the various other cans stored in cabinets and under sinks. I will not have to worry a whole lot about finances in the future or cleaning my own house myself.

"As for Elling," she says. "He's in custody and cooperating with the FBI. I just wish I had some news about your mother."

"Me too," I say. "You've done so much. I hate asking you, but could you . . ."

The detective chuckles. She doesn't smile much, as a rule. "Need a favor?"

"Well, yeah. Two, possibly?" I explain I want to make sure Dill Smith is not, in fact, my daddy. "And would you mind just one more little thing along the same line?" When I tell her, she says no problem.

The second request involves Evan. And me.

Evan shuffles in one day while Mim and Gramps take a break in the cafeteria. Head down, he drags up a chair. Sits for a long while. Hands lifeless, palms up on his legs.

"I'm sorry," he mumbles. I can hardly hear him. "I couldn't get loose. He tied me up in the cellar, said I'd stay out of his way this time."

I pretend I don't know he's there.

Evan is quiet for a long while. I fall asleep. When I wake up he's staring at me. "Anne?" he says.

"What."

"Nothing."

I turn my head away.

"What happened to you—it was my fault. I heard it all happening upstairs," he says, "and it—it made me freaking crazy. I was so afraid of him. If I couldn't get you to open the house, he was going to kill both of us." He's breathing hard. "I know. He almost killed you anyways." He gets up and walks around. "I should have kept him away and let him kill me."

He comes back. Stands a few feet from the bed. Smiles.

"My dad, he read the journal you wrote about me after he stole your computer. Turned it on, found *E/Jones*, read every word. Told me about it, how you trusted me. Liked me. Wanted us to be friends. He got a big laugh, pointed at me and said, 'Here's one stupid fool sponging off a rich girl. If she only knew. You'd be one hated sombitch.' He got that right.

"And then I read it, all those words you wrote about me. Words no one has ever said. Good words I'd never believe about myself. But you did."

He stands beside me now. I look at his hands, reaching out to grab the bed rail so tightly his knuckles go white. His sweatshirt sleeves slide up past his wrists. I see bloody welts where the rope cut his skin as he twisted to get free.

"I should have protected you." His eyes are deep pools of sadness. "I should have run away from him, told you, the police—someone." He turns sideways. "It's just . . . I didn't believe you cared, that anyone could. Until I read your words. Then it was too late. I don't blame you if you never want to see me again. But Anne, if you could forgive me . . ." His voice dwindles to nothing. He buries his face in his hands and sobs.

Tears slide out of my eyes and into my ears.

Gramps and Mim come back in the middle of it. I watch Gramps clamp a steel arm around Evan's shoulders. Mim walks to my bed and stands there like a guard. "How dare you show your face here?" she spits at him.

Gramps holds up a warning hand. "You know, kids," he says, "the best part of being young when something ugly like this happens: You got the rest of your life to make it right, and you two can if you want to."

I don't think I want to.

During my stay at the hospital, I have a few regular visitors.

Bianca and her mother spend hours with me. "Is dangerous, is crazy what you do," Mrs. Colon says every time, dabbing her eyes.

Bianca rolls her eyes. "Mama, it's 'did.' Anyway, she ever does it again, I'll kill her."

Lucy brings me a crossword puzzle book and a T-shirt from Band Day. "Brass section sucks again," she says.

Junior Vorhees even shows up with pink roses. "From the band," he says, "but I bought them. You look awful."

"Thanks," I say. "I feel pretty much the same way."

"When you coming back to school?"

I can't tell him never, so I smile and say nothing.

Evan doesn't come back. I have a lot of time to think about him. I try logic. Okay. He did stop Dill from molesting me during the first robbery. Evan must have read the note on his door about me staying at Mim's that night. So he believed the house would be empty when he and Dill went in. Because of my focus on Tal's shoes, I forgot about the pair just like Tal's I had bought Evan at the mall.

But Dill forced him to be his accomplice again. Evan was too afraid to do anything about it. When I think it over, I know he doesn't have a mean bone in his body, even though the way he was treated should have made him that way. The incident at the gas station. The fear in his little boy eyes. It's still there.

But he should have gone to the police.

For days, I have imaginary conversations with Evan. But nothing in my mind is settled. He's in my dreams, too. So is Dill, and I wake up screaming.

The night before I go to Mim and Gramps's I sit up in bed working a puzzle. My grandparents have gone home. Mim has made peace with Evan even though I haven't. He's staying in the stone house for now. Clearing away debris. Sweeping floors. Acting like a security guard. I tell Mim to have him put all of the cleaning and personal grooming cans together in a large, sealed box marked ANNE'S MISCELLANEOUS.

"Don't tell me you're taking over your mother's cleaning fixation."

"Could be," I say.

Something makes me look up. I drop my pencil. It rolls down the blanket and onto the floor.

Tal's father stands in the doorway.

FORTY-FOUR

HE wears a black suit. Pale blue shirt. Charcoal tie. He walks to my bed. Bends over, picks up the pencil, hands it to me. He still looks nothing like a lumberyard man.

I stare. It's Mr. Haynes, but it isn't. "Who are you?" I ask.

He laughs. Reaches into his jacket pocket and pulls out a badge and ID.

I study the photo. "Pete Davis, Deputy U.S. Marshal?"

He puts away his badge. "It's a long story, but basically, you have been under my protection since last summer. Most of the time another marshal and I watched your house from the apartment building across the street."

"Why?"

"To stop the felons trying to enter your home in an effort to find your mother. We did additional surveillance on other suspects crawling out of the woodwork and took several into custody. Somewhere else, the service was helping your mother into a new location."

"Wait! You know where she is?" I practically jump out of bed. Kills my ribs.

"Not specifically, but she's safe. Didn't Elling tell you she joined the Witness Protection Program?"

"Then it's true?"

Mr. Davis pulls up a chair, sits, crosses one leg over the other. "Yes. I know he turned out to be a lemon, but your mother had us call him a few weeks back to get her affairs in order for you and to transfer funds once she's established in her new identity. We added that, for your safety, you would have to leave Centerville soon and his services as your mother's lawyer would be terminated. That's all we told him."

I nod. Elling must have seen Mom's money as a banquet ready for a one-man feast.

"We did our best to protect you, Anne." Mr. Davis looks uncomfortable. "But for one thing, those blasted trees blocked your house. To top that, we knew nothing about Dill Smith. He was a wild, bad card."

"I know." Something jabbed at a memory. "What happened outside my house that one night?"

"What night was that?" Mr. Davis pushes his chair backward and stands. He paces around the room jingling coins and keys in his pocket. I wish he'd sit.

"I heard punching and running. All kinds of noise."

He stops. "Oh, yes. Another marshal and I tackled a suspect from Chicago trying to get in. He wasn't the first or last. We caught most of them between one and four AM. Not a whole lot of shut-eye."

I think of how scared I was that time. Good thing I slept through the others.

But Mom, safe!

My hand self-consciously travels to the apparatus holding

my jaw shut. I haven't been able to face my face in the mirror yet.

Mr. Davis chooses his next words carefully. "In light of what happened with Smith and the robbery of your home, Evan Jones could face charges."

"I won't testify against him," I say. "No way. He deserves a break after living with Dill Smith most of his life—you know, the Stockholm syndrome?"

Mr. Davis does something surprising. He points a finger at me. "If you had stayed out of that house, we could have caught Smith ourselves."

I hate it when someone points at me.

So I say, "If you had let me in about what was going on in the first place, I might not be sitting here." I fiddle with my blanket. "Why didn't you tell me about my mother? I know how to keep a secret."

The marshal's mouth turns way down. "The less you knew, the better. We wanted to make sure any felon who came to town looking for her and seeking you out would notice your genuine fear of never seeing your mother alive again. We were setting the stage for your mother's and your departure.

"Then came the slipup with the body. You were supposed to be told it was beyond recognition, but your mother talked us into allowing you to find out she was alive. So we produced a substitute corpse. That was a trip."

I remember the policeman at the morgue telling me not to react, merely to nod. The chilling joy when I saw the unfamiliar face.

Mr. Davis's voice sounds lighter. "Bet you wonder about that crummy house in Westfield."

"Yeah."

"We use the place for various operations and stayed there a few months because it was closer to Centerville than Springfield. My 'wife' the day you visited is an FBI agent." Mr. Davis pauses and looks behind him at the door, then back at me..Grins. "Aren't you the slightest bit curious about another member of my team? Someone you knew as Tal Haynes?"

My breath catches in my throat, causing an odd squeak.

"Is that a yes?"

I give him a small nod.

"He's my nephew, Sam Davis. Sonny's a fine young man, a recent high school graduate who's thinking about becoming a marshal himself. So when this assignment came up, I said to him, 'How'd you like to test the waters and help out a real nice girl?' Sonny, come on in here."

Behind him in the doorway appears the person I never thought I'd see again. He wears jeans and a Cubs T-shirt. Blue and white sneakers. His hair is shorter, darker. Nearly black. "Hi, Anne," he says. Same gorgeous smile.

"Sonny earned his pay. Regular team member. He reported back to us. We had FBI agent Gwen Pierce meet with him now and then with updates and other information."

Gwen, aka Shelley. I was right after all.

Mr. Davis raises his eyebrows and puts his hands behind his back. "You do realize that Sonny, well, had to play the part of the boyfriend who keeps the girlfriend interested?"

I blush and pick at a hangnail. "I do now."

He chuckles. "We told him up front he had to behave himself around you. No hanky-panky. Kinda hard for him, methinks."

No doubt my face is now one shade away from a ripe tomato ready to explode.

Sam, looking annoyed, gestures at the door. "Uncle Pete, could I . . . we . . ."

"Could you what?" He glances around. Then a bulb lights up. "Oh, right." He claps his hands. "I'm going out in the hall for a few minutes. Get a cup of coffee."

Sam waits until he leaves, then sits beside me. "My uncle can be a little dense."

"Dense? What about me? You must have had a great time pretending to be debonair band boy," I say, "stopping, starting up again, disappearing."

"Oh." He looks embarrassed. "After I'd been hanging around you a couple of weeks, the guys in charge of the operation called me in and said the situation was under control, so they wouldn't need me anymore. But a few days later everything fell apart for your mother. 'Go back to Lincoln,' they told me. 'Make sure Anne likes your company.'"

I try to laugh as though I don't care. "Right," I say, and turn my head away.

"You think it was fun for me? It wasn't, not like that. I didn't want to lie to you." Sam clears his throat. "My job was to get to know you so I could enter your place, check it out, and use the security system code your mother provided if my uncle told me to go in by myself."

I remember the first time "Tal" came over, peeked in different rooms. He was casing the joint!

"How did they arrest my mother?" I ask. "I mean, was your uncle there, and did he tell you what she said?"

Sam looks confused. "Arrest? No one arrested her. Uncle Pete said that six years ago she went to the FBI and offered a deal they couldn't refuse. Your mother worked hard as an informant, but someone—she was involved with so many thugs—caught on and blew the whistle. That's when the marshals arranged her disappearance. It took longer than they thought."

"Then Mom isn't a criminal?"

"Nope."

She had left the hero part out of her letter to me. I whoop, then gasp at the pain. "All those times she risked her life. But before, she—well—was involved—with—"

"Yeah, I heard. In that case, usually everything a person gets illegally is seized. Uncle Pete said she got them to forgive a lot of stuff because of what she knew and could do for them. Plus, she'd kept up on her taxes."

Yes, that would be my mother. Careful. I reach for my cup and straw. Sam takes it from the table and holds it while I siphon water through my teeth. I'm ecstatic about Mom.

"Did you hear about my run-in with J.J. San Marino and this list he wanted me to find for him? He told me my mother was really good at hiding things." Especially when it came to keeping me guessing, I think.

"Yeah, I heard." He laughs. "I understand you have a dangerous set of attack legs, too, and a garbage can as weapon of choice."

"I found the list he wanted on a tape. A bunch of names, numbers, weird words. I burned it."

"It's probably a spreadsheet of money-laundering establishments, hit men, crooks with MOs she got from the FBI—a study guide, so to speak, in code. With the list he could blackmail other cons. Your mother probably baited him with it sometime before she was outed. Man, my mom makes great lasagna. Your mom?" He shakes his head. "She's something else."

"You don't know the half of it."

We're quiet a few moments. Then I ask him. "The money

in the Popsicle box the night we went to my house and I got sick. You didn't take it, did you? When I saw you punch in the code, I thought–"

"That I stole it later. That's logical. Yeah, I took it."

"You–"

"The cash is at the Springfield agency. My guess is you'll get it sometime after the first of the year."

I struggle to sit up. "But when you disappeared that night–"

"I entered in the new code without thinking, a stupid slipup, but one that killed off Tal Haynes, Lincoln High student. I could never have explained away that one to you. I told Uncle Pete, and he sent me home. When I heard about what happened with Smith, it made me sick. I never thought you'd go back into that house after the experience with J.J. Should have known better. Anne, is there anything you're afraid of?"

I bow my head, expecting all the emotions I've stuffed away–fear, love, a sense of abandonment–to creep back. But they don't. I'm surprised, even a little sad. "Then the whole thing for you was a job," I say.

"Why would I come to see you now if it was just a job?"

"Because your uncle made you."

He smiles. "I've been waiting a long time to clear things up."

I nod. "I'm glad you're not a bad boy after all. You really think you'll become a marshal?"

"Yeah. After college." He stands. Puts his hands in his pockets. "I guess you realize you have to go away now," he says, "and no one can know where you are, not me, not Uncle Pete, not anyone."

"They told me that."

"You and your mother might be in danger for a long time. No one from your past can visit or call you." He lowers his head for what seems like forever, then raises it and looks steadily into my eyes. "So that's the way it's going down. I don't think it'll be easy."

"I'm ready for it." I muster up as positive a smile as I can, dry lips, stitches, and all. "Thank you for protecting me," I say. "You were a much better friend to me than I was to you."

"And you're the bravest girl I've ever met." He walks toward the door. Turns. "I'll remember you, Anne. For the rest of my life."

FORTY-FIVE

I feel at least seventy the next day when the nurse rolls my wheelchair to Gramps and Mim's car.

Through the holidays I rest and walk short distances around the neighborhood. Completely avoid the stone house. My new deputy U.S. marshal guarded me at the hospital and now is nearby. Bianca is fascinated by my battle scars. "You are woman! Hear you roar!" she says with a fist in the air.

For weeks, I wonder what Detective Rodriguez will find out about Evan and me.

How will I react?

After New Year's, I get a call from the detective. "Smith's day in court is set for March fifth," she says. "And something else: It's raining money your way. The Springfield FBI is sending over a whole lot of thousand-dollar bills for you originally from, is this right, a polka-dotted refrigerator?"

I laugh. "Yeah, my cool cash. I found out my mom's okay."

"I got wind of that myself. By the way, you'll be glad to know you won't be taking the stand against your father, only against a felon named Dill Smith. As far as the other thing you had me check out, here goes."

After I put down the phone, my eyes fill up.

I know the truth now. It takes my breath away.

Owen Elling eventually admits transferring a lot of Mom's money to overseas banks and hiding her assets at his home in Middleboro. He even confesses to searching inside the stone house once for cash but giving up. Mom was really something, the way she hid money. Hey, so was I for being able to discover it. As she said at the end of her letter, "Think hard. I know you *can*." Even with a purpose, her puns are the worst.

Gramps and Mim know I'm leaving Centerville and going into hiding, but I'm not allowed to tell them Penny's still alive. They get the deed to their house. Half of the proceeds from the sale of mine, which I'm glad to unload, goes into their bank account. Good-bye, stone house!

Before it sells, I walk by. The morning breeze is sweet with the smell of lilac. Sun warms my bare arms. I see the flowers Evan and I planted peeking through the soil. In a way, they remind me of the two of us emerging from the dark, growing toward a new life.

Our first conversations after the hospital remind me of a car with transmission problems jerking and stumbling down the road. But eventually, our awkwardness dissolves. After the trial on a windy March afternoon, I tell Evan, not charged with a crime, though he came close, that my mother is still alive.

"I'm going to live with her," I say. He nods. Looks away. "I wish you could, too."

"Not me."

I nudge his arm. "Why?"

"I don't belong," he says. "I'd screw everything up. Always have."

"Being a victim of an evil man is not screwing up."

He puts up both hands. "It's over. I don't want to think about it or talk about it."

"Me either."

Later, we sit on the floor, and I open all of the cans he had put in a big box. "The money goes in the safety-deposit box for now," I say.

He picks up a stack of thousand-dollar bills. "The one thing I remember learning back in grade school is that these things aren't in circulation anymore. How did your ma get so many of them?"

"I don't know. She told me once she had invested. Guess she bought and collected them."

Later we arrive at the bank. I walk with the pouch to the employee and give her my key. Soon I've put the package in the box and taken out the only item in the container. A manila envelope. The last of my mother's trail of clues, something she acquired after finishing her letter to me. She had never put in cremation certificates, as she said the night we went to Mama Leone's when she gave me the key. Another one of her odd jokes to keep me out of the box until the very end.

"Let's get some rhubarb pie," I say when we're in the Jeep. "I've never had any, have you?"

"Yeah. It's sour."

The waitress at Redman's tells us they are out of rhubarb

pie. We order apple à la mode instead and sit in the back booth under a poster of a cowboy shooting a buffalo. I feel sorry for the buffalo.

Evan rests his chin on both hands. "I guess you'll be taking off soon," he says.

I nod. My stomach turns at what I am about to tell him. "When Detective Rodriguez asked to swab your cheek," I say, "it wasn't to rule you out as a suspect. It was to determine a fact, and it did."

"What did she find out?"

"How well do you like Dill Smith as a father?"

"Take a guess."

"He's not your father."

Evan sits expressionless. Then he shakes his head. "You mean all those years, years of nothing but—"

"I know. Did he ever tell you why he was trying to extort money from my mother?"

"He didn't say anything—only gave orders. Be there. Do this or else. Do that. No reasons. We moved to Centerville to get money from your ma. It was my job to keep an eye on you at school. That's all he said to do at first. When me and you first met, I didn't know what his plan was. He's had so many as long as I can remember, but when he found out I was actually staying with you, he said it was a sign that he deserved what he could take.

"Then when he heard your ma was dead, he got all excited and made me talk you into opening the house. If I wouldn't, he said he'd kill me first, then go after you." He runs his hand through his hair. "I did hide from him. Whenever I could. But his talent—I guess you know—was finding people. He never quit. Like a guy in a nightmare."

"Exactly," I say.

We sit for several minutes in silence while we finish our pie and ice cream. I wish I hadn't eaten it. I feel sick. Evan picks up tiny bits of crust from the table. Deposits them on an unused napkin.

"Remember when you said you had a sister with hair the same color as mine?" I ask.

"Yeah, but she was a baby. Ma did something with her, sent her to a relative to live, I guess. She was pretty young. I was young, too, but Ma had a photo of the two of us. I guess it's the picture I remember. Why are you bringing that up?"

I place the manila envelope on the table and slide out its contents. "What was your sister's name?"

"Maryann," he says. "It was written on the back of the photo. Maryann and Bertie."

I place the birth certificate in front of him. "Does this look right?" I ask.

"Yeah. Maryann Jones. Mother: Eleanor Jones. Cook County, father unknown." He laughs. "What are you doing with it?"

"Penny, my adoptive mother, got it for me."

He looks at me, then at the certificate, then back at me. His voice wobbles. "Whoa, are you serious?"

I slide the document back into the envelope. "The DNA test proves Dill is not your father or mine, and the certificate makes it official. Eleanor Jones is my birth mother." I watch him closely.

His hands are spread out flat on the table. He is staring up at the buffalo. "And I'm your brother!" His eyes go wild, and he looks around as if he's going to bolt. "I'm as stupid as they come."

I put one hand out near his. "No, wait, Evan. Dill is not

your father or mine. That's true. And Eleanor is my mother. But she . . . Eleanor is not *your* mother."

He turns to face me. "What? I don't under—"

"The DNA, yours and mine, have nothing in common. We don't match. So you can't be Eleanor's son."

I see the confusion, hurt in his eyes. He raises himself and moves away from me to the corner of the booth. Fades. Sinks like a waterlogged rowboat. "Where did I come from, then? I don't belong to Dill. Don't belong to Eleanor. What a laugh. I don't even belong to jerks." His voice is miserable. "Who am I?"

"You're Evan," I say. "I have no idea where you came from, but I know you belong to someone."

"Who?" he asks in a hoarse voice. "Who could I ever belong to?"

I slide over next to him. Put my head on his shoulder. "Me."

FORTY-SIX

TWO days before leaving Centerville, I visit Bianca and her mom. I promise to call as soon as I'm settled, a total lie. I want Bianca to know something, though. She walks with me to my Jeep. As I open the door I say, "Don't tell anyone, but Tal ended up being one of the good guys. His uncle's a U.S. marshal who recruited him to keep me safe."

Her eyes get all wide. "Annie, what a relief. I'm really glad because of the way you felt about him. Do you still?"

I smile and shake my head. "I thought if I ever saw him again, the whole love thing would fly right back into my lame brain. But it didn't. He couldn't let anything happen between us because he was doing his job."

Bianca raises her thick eyebrows. "You can't say you didn't try to break down the wall."

I nod and grin. "Yeah, but it's hard to get through steel. I respect what he did. Not at the time."

She holds on to the door. Pulls on the handle. "And

Evan? What about him? What will he do now? Has he left Centerville?"

"He's staying in the Brownstone Apartments on Elm." I leave off the part about foisting money on him to help him survive. "I'm hoping he'll go for his GED at the community center."

"It's Evan, isn't it?"

"What do you mean?"

"That's why your feelings for Tal changed."

I don't answer her.

She pats my arm. "Wow. Now you have to leave him, too. Life is so unfair." She looks down. Kicks the pavement. "I'm not an idiot. You're never coming back. I mean, this is it. We won't see each other or talk again." She raises her eyes. Tears slip out. Run down her face. "Right?"

"Yeah," I say. I grab her and hug her tighter than I've ever hugged anyone. "Doesn't mean I won't think of you every day for the rest of my life."

She's sobbing. "Me too. But not talk to you? That sucks."

"Maybe when we both are like in our forties and all of this has gone away."

Bianca smiles. The same silly smile she wore the first time I saw her. "Someday seems an awfully long time from now. But what about Evan?"

I shake my head. "When I'm gone will you look in on him sometimes?"

I watch Bianca and the farmhouse disappear in my rearview mirror as I drive away. My eyes are so full of tears the road is blurred like rain. It's not fair. There has to be a way we can write to one another.

• • •

Gramps, Mim, and I spend the night reminiscing and playing canasta. Before we go to bed, Mim opens a closet and lifts out a soft package covered in tissue. "Your grandpa took a few stitches himself," she tells me. "When you sleep under this, think of our arms wrapped around you."

I tear off the paper and hold up my grown-up quilt, white with blue and yellow stars and beams that reach all the way to the binding. "Oh, guys!" I say. "You two are the best."

"Champ, you've been in our hearts for sixteen and a half years." Gramps is crying. "What will we do without you?"

"Herman, you old sappy fool," Mim says. Then she breaks down.

I don't cry.

In six months they will join us. In the middle of the night, marshals will come quietly, and Mim and Gramps will slip out with them and disappear. Just as I am about to.

I had sent Mom a message through a marshal.

I'll live with you as long as Mim and Gramps can come.

My deputy marshal reported back: affirmative.

It's ten-thirty. I'm ready for bed when Mim knocks on the door. "Evan's here to see you," she says.

I pull on my clothes. Look at my reflection in the mirror. Touch the small scar, still red, below my right eye. When I enter the living room I see Gramps with a hand on Evan's shoulder. "I know a heck of a lot of folks," he says, "and I'll talk to some of them about hiring you."

I clear my throat. Gramps gives a little wave and leaves the room.

Evan turns to me. His face changes, and he shifts his feet. Puts his hands behind his back.

"Come on," I say. We go outside. I hear Mim through the screen door reminding me how late it is. "All right," I call back to her.

I sit on the top step and lean against the railing. Evan stands, hands in pockets, at the bottom.

"I'm leaving day after tomorrow," I say. "Kind of scary and exciting at the same time. I'll even have a new name."

"What is it?"

"They haven't told me yet. No one can know anyway. So. Are you going to be okay?"

Evan doesn't move. The night is chilly and dark and quiet with one streetlight glowing at the end of the block.

"I still wish you were going with me even though you can't. Anyway, I was wondering. Can Zorro stay with you? It would be a relief to me."

"Yeah, that'd be okay. I'll take good care of Zor Boy." Evan walks a little way into the yard, then comes halfway back. "Your ma," he says. "You told me she started out without a dime, then worked her way through college. That's something."

"She's amazing. But not perfect."

"Yeah, well, who is? Anyways, I was thinking if I could get my GED, go to college, then figure out what to do with my life, maybe. . ." He turns away from me. I can barely see his outline.

"Maybe what?"

He doesn't answer.

I get up and walk to him. "Yes, definitely college. You can do it. I'll give you moral support, 'cause guess what? When

I'm gone, you and I can write to each other care of the marshals. It goes like this: we send letters to the field office, and they deliver them. No one can trace them."

He shakes his head.

For the first time tonight, I really look at him. He's dressed up. Nice khaki pants. White shirt with a collar. Glossy hair. Bangs falling over one side of his forehead. Flushed face.

I move closer. "Why don't you want to write me?" I ask.

"You know how bad I am at it."

"Do you think I care?"

He shrugs.

"If you don't want to write words, draw your thoughts. Or we could work on the comic book. That would be fun. Sending it back and forth."

Evan smiles for the first time. "Maybe. Yeah, okay. We could do that."

"Think I could be a character in it?"

"Sure, you're the princess the captive guy hopes for when he's in the dungeon."

"And—um—are you the captive guy?"

Evan reaches out, his hands barely touching my arms. "Why do you think I want to get an education? If I'm not a nobody, maybe someday we could—"

"Yes." I put one hand over his heart. "Maybe."

The porch light comes on. Mim opens the door. "Anne, it's after midnight."

We move apart. Evan mumbles something.

"Okay, Mim. Coming," I say.

My last night in Centerville. I'm sitting in Evan's apartment eating the dinner we've made together. Macaroni and cheese, cut-up cantaloupe, lettuce wedges with Caesar dressing. The studio apartment came furnished. Kitchen, bedroom, living room in one compact space. Bathroom the size of a shoebox next to the closet. I brought along a pale yellow candle for the table, where it now sits dripping and flickering.

Evan and I don't talk much. But he looks at me as if he wants to. Afterward, we clean up, then move to the small brown sofa. Zorro's grooming himself on an arm of the adjacent chair.

"See how happy he is?" I say. "He's forgotten me already." We watch the cat for a while.

"Oh, listen. If you need any help with GED stuff," I tell Evan, "call Bianca. She said she'll meet you anytime you need her. Let me give you her phone number. I'll get some paper." I reach for my purse.

"Anne, I love you something terrible." His voice is low.

I raise my head. "I know." I look back at my purse. Rummage around in it. "Do you have paper? I can't seem to find any."

He moves closer and touches my shoulder. I'm in his arms then, and we're standing up. And I say, listening to his heart, my face against his chest, "You've got to gain some weight. Promise." He says, "I will," and I'm crying because this is both the beginning and the end of something I know is real. Something that took a long time to bloom but is so tender I can hardly stand it. I try to remember when it started but can't. Evan's spirit, his shyness, his sweet nature, despite all he put up with, mean everything to me now.

He steps back slightly so he can see my face. I look at his. At his beautiful green eyes full of love. For me. Then he finishes what he started in the guesthouse. This time I kiss him back. Because I love him, too.

• • •

Early in the morning I ride with U.S. Marshal Paul Kingston to the airport. I've dyed my hair black. We will fly west to join my mother. Maybe now that her flights are grounded, she'll write the great American novel.

Somehow, I know it'll never happen.

I think of everything I am leaving behind. Bianca and Centerville will always be in my heart. Evan? Someday, somehow, we'll meet again. We made that vow to each other last night. But Mom and I will be reunited soon. That's the important thing now, and I can't wait to hear the rest of her saga, to meet the real Penny.

Strange. I think I'll like Diane Stillman.

I also have a few pointed questions to ask, and this time she can't go running off. Even though she did it for me, money ruled her life and just about ruined mine. My own future, I decide, will be about something different. Something much more important.

Starting today.

ACKNOWLEDGMENTS

Many thanks to my agent, Stephanie Lehmann, for all her help and support, and to Elaine Koster of the Elaine Koster Literary Agency; to my editor, Claudia Gabel, for her enthusiasm and guidance; to Lillian Wong, Judy Wallace, and above all, Jody Davis; to writing group members Anitha Weiss, Nicole DeLeon, Carrie McKirchy, Janet Burrel, Janine Weyers, and especially Rita Buhrman for socking it to me; to my parents, Loren and Bette Gamash, who taught me with laughter and song, in our modest home down a dusty road, to love the written word.